The
AMERICANS
CAME

PATRICIA GILL

PORTLAND • OREGON
INKWATERPRESS.COM

This is a work of fiction. The events described here are imaginary. The settings and characters are fictitious and do not represent specific places or living or dead people. Any resemblance is entirely coincidental.

Ad familiam cura futuri.

7/14/07

With all good wishes —

Patricia Gill

Christiansted, St-Croix

ACKNOWLEDGEMENTS

Many thanks to the members of the Writer's Circle of Saint Croix or their patience, encouragement and generosity in sharing their expertise. Ken Floyd's eagle-eyed vision and aim for perfection in editing is much appreciated.

CHAPTER ONE

Stephen found relief from the early afternoon sun by sharing the shade of a palm tree between the sea and Strand Street with a tall, stout black woman whose face, turned away from him, was half-hidden by a broad-brimmed hat placed securely on top of a madras kerchief. If she sensed his presence, she did not turn to acknowledge it but continued to stare up at the Danish Flag flying from the tower of Fort Frederik at the end of the street. The woman's strong straight back and the defiant stance were familiar. He was almost certain his tree-sharer was Beulah Heyliger and the possibility filled him with the same awe he had felt as a child entering her bakeshop.

When she did turn to face him their eyes met at the same level. Beulah was no longer a black giant frowning down on a terrified child who was afraid that the coin for the family bread might slip through his sweaty fingers. He had dropped it once and he still remembered Beulah's scolding as he rushed to the doorsill to retrieve it.

"Jus' stop scarin' my hens, scramblin' 'bout like a land crab. Dey'll stop layin' eggs, and den where'll you get your cakes, de ones your mudda likes so much?"

Stephen's mother no longer ate cake, but listening to Beulah he felt like the child he had once been.

"It's young Master Stephen, isn't it?" she asked. After Stephen nodded to confirm the guess, she continued, "You 'member me don' you? I'm Beulah. Your fadda tol' me you back. You grow a lot. Just 'bout tall as me. You'd be taller if you stood up straight 'stead a leanin' agin' dat tree. Look at your fadda up dere on de balcony. Now dere's a man who stan' straight. Fine, upstandin' man, your fadda. He does look real good in his funeral suit. It's not a funeral, a flag comin'down. Just as sad, dough, in a way."

"What's so sad about a flag coming down?" Stephen said. "We voted for it. We wanted it. We wanted to become Americans. And that's not a *funeral* suit."

"Who voted for it? Not me. You forget who kin vote here. Dey tol' me you was a lawyer now. Some lawyer. Don'even know de law. Got a mout' on you, dough. Always did."

Stephen, with an effort, decided to keep his offending mouth shut. Besides, Beulah's attention had wandered to the local band, now playing the Star-Spangled Banner as the American flag slithered up the rope to replace the descending Danish one

"Play nice, don' dey?" she said. The uniformed group on the freshly painted white gazebo in front of the Fort was playing their wind instruments and banging their drums energetically.

"Very nice," Stephen replied, surprised that it was true. Despite the heat and the constrictions of the tight, high-necked braided jackets, the twelve middle-aged black men produced a better-sounding version of the Star Spangled Banner than the well-rehearsed student band at his Harvard Law School graduation.

"I hear the Americans don' like us black people," Beulah said.

Stephen hesitated. "I saw no signs of it at Harvard," he finally said.

"Lawyer, liar," Beulah said. "Well, we'll see. Come by me shop. I'll give you a loaf of nice fresh bread as a graduation present."

"Thanks. I'd like that. The best bread I ever tasted."

"That's why my business doin' so good. I'm a successful business woman but I didn't get no invite to the party your fadda's givin' for all dem important people up dere lookin' down on us."

"But local business people were invited. I know. My father insisted upon it when they asked him to give the reception for the Navy. I saw some invitations myself. Ralph Henry. John Hawes. Perhaps yours got lost in delivery."

"Ralph Henry!" Beulah tossed her head and clicked her tongue against the roof of her mouth. "I may have flour on me hands, but he got ink on his. I read his paper every morning. I even sell dem in my store. John Hawes? My business bigger dan his. Wha' does he do but sell a few provisions, half of dem rotten. I'm surprised at your fadda, forgettin'me. It ain't like him to forget Beulah."

"My fault," said Stephen. "It's all my fault. It was my responsibility to check the list. Please come to the reception, Miss Beulah. I have to go now. I promised Mother I would see that everything was set up properly. The naval officers are very prompt. Father warned me."

"Dey don' go by Cruzan time," Beulah laughed, restored to good humor. "I'll be dere as soon as I can. I goin'to change to me funeral clothes. Don'look so. I jus' foolin'.

I goin' to wear me church clothes, good enough for God, good enough for de Americans. Your mudda won't be dere? Still doin'poorly, is she? She missed you real bad, all de years you was away. Your brudda, he try to take your place, but you de one she dotes on. Big help to your fadda, your brudda Mark. But your mudda…poor woman."

"The Navy is bringing in new doctors…and building a new hospital."

"Jus'for de white people?"

"Of course not."

"At least de Danes give us a hospital. And doctors. And train our local girls to be nurses."

"I must go. I'll tell Father you're coming."

"Tell me cousin Ralph I'm comin'. Didn't you know he was me cousin? So high and mighty, him bein' invited and not me. All you white people 'fraid of Ralph. Not me."

She's right, Stephen thought as he walked up past the shorefront warehouses to the Markham property, the three-story white house decorated with carved wood balconies. The style, known as "Frederiksted Gingerbread", camouflaged the utilitarian purpose of the first floor offices but was in keeping with the interior courtyard of palms, climbing vines and flowering bushes.

He hoped the Navy would be favorably impressed by the attractive building but kept reminding himself that externals were not enough. Just a few years away from the island and he had almost forgotten the basic rules of maintaining social harmony on Saint Croix. Never forget blood or acquired relatives and stay on the right side of Ralph Henry. Stephen recalled his grandfather's oft-repeated tales of the Labor Riots of 1878 and his father's insistence on politeness and respect, a lecture repeated a few days after his return home.

His father had reminded him that the Markhams had always been merchants, business men who sold plows to plantation owners, machetes to the cane-growers and ink to the newspaper editor. Good men were those who paid their bills on time. A labor leader like Ralph Henry, who published a newspaper that everybody read, was a valued customer because he had never asked for a discount although he often received one.

To cut short the familiar lecture, Stephen had asked his father what Ralph Henry was likely to write about the transfer of the islands from Denmark to the United States.

"I can't predict that." Cedric Markham was not a tall man but he did stand very straight, as Beulah had noted. He spoke slowly, clearly, thoughtfully and people tended to listen to what he had to say.

"I wonder how the Naval Administration is going to treat him," Stephen said.

"My only responsibility right now is to see that the Transfer ceremonies take place smoothly, that the band plays on cue as the American flag goes up and that the basic etiquette of gentlemen is observed as the Danes relinquish power. At least, Captain Warner finally agreed to my inviting some of the local people when he found out that the Danes considered it correct procedure. This March 31st will be a day to forget as far as I'm concerned. It's been a nightmare with no precedent to follow, no real rules for protocol. I can't predict what the Naval Administration will do. I have no influence with the Americans."

Stephen was suspicious of the disclaimer. His father always had influence. Still, he was relieved that the official ceremonies had gone smoothly and gratified to find that the courtyard of the Markham town house had been decorated with flowers, just enough of his mother's hybrid hibiscus plants to provide an attractive tropical background for an elegant reception. The silver punch bowl and crystal glasses reflected the bright colors of the flowers. Almost-ripe coconuts had been carefully slashed from the palms lest one fall on an official head and the seductive aroma of nutmeg and vanilla hovered over the punch. Stephen had heard that the American Navy liked Cruzan rum and he hoped it was true.

The uniformed group arrived, closely followed by the local guests, men in either dark or white linen suits, the women in ornate colorful dresses and wide-brimmed hats. Stephen obeyed his mother's request by observing everyone closely in order to recount to her later the most detailed description of clothes, behavior, everything.

His father interrupted his concentration by beckoning him over to meet Captain Warner. "Our new Naval Administrator," Mr. Markham said. "This is my younger son, Stephen. You've already met Mark."

"It will be quite cool in another hour," Stephen said, noting that wilted collar of the Captain's uniform. "May I get you a drink, sir?"

Captain Warner, a man of medium height, gray-haired and gray-eyed, had a stance as steady as his gaze, his feet planted firmly on the bricks of the courtyard as if the ground might suddenly sway. *A confident man,* Stephen thought, *used to issuing orders and having them obeyed without question. I wonder how he and father will get along.*

As if to belie his authoritarian manner, the Administrator lapsed into informal, conversational speech. "In a moment, in a moment. I always sweat like this when a ceremony is over. All those years in Panama, same thing, over and over, every damn time. Nice and calm and dry while they're making speeches and playing music, but afterwards…well, at least you sweat *afterwards*, my wife always says. She apologizes for not being here, Mr. Markham, but the sun, you know, doctor forbids it, too many years in the tropics. Well, well," he said as he turned his attention to Stephen, "your father is a fortunate man, to have two able sons by his side to help him in his business. And he tells me that you are a lawyer as well."

"Yes, sir, I am a lawyer."

"Not much action in the law, is there? My son's in the Navy. Just one boy, that's all we have, but he's done us proud. Second in his class at the Academy. I was hoping to have him here for the ceremony, but with this war business in Europe…" Captain Warner shrugged and from under his bushy gray eyebrows shrewd eyes appraised Stephen's face carefully. "Your father tells me his sons are American citizens. If he hadn't told me, I would have picked you for a Dane."

"My mother is Danish, sir."

"So your father tells me. Nevertheless, you studied law in America, at Harvard, a good school, a good school. Prefer the University of Virginia myself, but Harvard's a good school."

"I think so, sir."'

"Your father has volunteered your services, nothing complicated, you understand, but military procedures are one thing and civilian law is another, as I told them when they appointed me Administrator here. I don't know why they don't come right out and say the Navy is in command and let me run this place like a tight ship. But no, I've been advised not to offend the civilian populace. Orders are orders. I will need your services."

"What services, sir? I didn't know anything about this."

"Well, I guess your father didn't get much of a chance to tell you, since I just spoke to him about it before the ceremony started. Don't worry, it won't take up much of your time, you can still work for your father. All of us in the Navy know that the most important thing in these outposts is discipline. Now discipline I *do* know about. I'm a Navy man. I didn't spend all those years in Panama for nothing. Let them know who is in control right away. Hard work rewarded and laziness not tolerated. Your father understands that, or he wouldn't have been so successful in business here."

"I'm sure my father did not recommend me as a disciplinarian," Stephen said, glancing at his father and reminding himself that an official reception was not the place for a family quarrel. "What *did* he recommend me for?"

"Well, I'm afraid we're going to have a *big* war to worry about and I don't want any *small*, annoying disturbances. Your father says you were born and brought up here, know the customs, the people and the traditions. You've also spent some time in America, studied American law. I want you to figure out what the friction points might be and avoid them, just don't let them happen. I want to concentrate on the things I'm supposed to accomplish, clean up this fever spot, get rid of the damn mosquitoes, get the hospital functioning properly, train the local people, if we can, in some of the lower levels of administration just in case of attack when the military are needed for the important things. Not much chance of attack, in my opinion, but we must always be prepared."

"I'm afraid I don't quite understand what you want me to do."

"You're a lawyer and as I told them up in Washington, law is law, and the laws of the United States are the best in the world, but all I know is the Navy way. Still, we had a few experiences in Panama that I don't want to see repeated here if it can be avoided. I need a local man I can trust to run interference for me, as they say in football."

Stephen refrained from saying he had never played football as he watched Captain Warner replace the handkerchief wet from wiping his face with a crisp, dry one from his hip pocket and breathe deeply of the cooler evening air.

"That's a nice sea breeze. Well, Mr. Markham, there were some people you wanted me to meet. I'll see you soon, young man."

Stephen, too annoyed for casual conversation, sought out his brother Mark, who was standing unobtrusively in an isolated corner, half-hidden by bougainvillea.

"You've met the new Administrator, that Navy captain? What a pompous ass! What does he take me for? He could have waited a few days before he invited me to be a scapegoat. I guess he thinks I didn't learn anything at law school, if I didn't recognize a ploy like that. And Father went along with it."

"You exaggerate, Stephen, as usual." Mark smiled and Stephen felt his anger ebb. Mark's smile was their mother's smile and he had inherited her equable disposition as well.

"Come on," Mark continued. "It's a good party. Mother will be pleased. No one's getting drunk or cussing anyone else out. The Americans seem to be enjoying our conch fritters and meat patties."

Stephen noticed that Beulah Heyliger, who had stationed herself in the center of the courtyard, was talking in normal tones and smiling. He confessed to Mark, "Father forgot to invite Beulah, so I did."

Mark explained that their father had agonized over the guest list, reluctant to offend any of his local friends. The Governor had sent over word from Saint Thomas that most of the naval officers were "southerners who should not be made to feel uncomfortable" and recommended that the number of local people invited be very few. Mr. Markham had finally consulted his friend Father Morrow, the Rector of the Anglican Church, about the guest list.

"He always manages to drag in the church somehow," Stephen said. He noticed that Father Morrow, standing next to Beulah Heyliger, and sipping a rum punch, looked relaxed, not worrying about who was invited and who wasn't. "The Rector looks more like a scarecrow than ever. Englishmen enjoy pomp and circumstance and uniforms. I've never heard him say anything good about Americans, and now he's greeting them like long-lost brothers.'"

"The threat of war has changed the way a lot of Europeans feel about Americans. Besides, he's just being affable and polite. Not a bad choice when nobody really knows how to behave when one flag comes down and another goes up."

"Well, then, I guess he's doing what we've always been taught to do. When in doubt, be polite," Stephen said.

"Father didn't invite Beulah because he was afraid she might have a few rums and begin shouting things offensive to Americans," Mark said. "But Father Morrow has kept her busy chatting and it's worked out well. I'm glad you invited her. It'll be all over Frederiksted tomorrow that she was here, she'll tell everyone who comes into the bakeshop, and that's everyone. You were right. You always are."

"I just happened to run into her on the street during the ceremony."

"If I know Beulah, she saw you coming. Look over there. According to the timetable he gave us, Captain Warner will be leaving within ten minutes and I can start shooing people out of here. So keep your eye on Beulah until then. "

Soothed by his brother's flattery, Stephen went over to join Father Morrow and Beulah.

"So glad you both could come. Could I get you something to eat or drink?"

Beulah ignored the question. "De Americans takin'over de church as well as de government. In Puerto Rico dey won't even let us natives into the House of God. Next ting dey'll be chasin'us off our own island."

"Don't talk nonsense, Beulah," Father Morrow said. "The only change will be legal jurisdiction. You're a lawyer now, Stephen. I'm sure you understand."

"Not really."

Stephen listened politely as Father Morrow explained church law to him. Now that the Danish West Indies had officially become the Virgin Islands of the United States, the Church of England would cede jurisdiction of its mission churches to the Episcopal Church of America. But Beulah had nothing to fear, Father Morrow insisted, because Bishop Hutson in Antigua had proclaimed himself unwilling to yield to any changes in canon law that might jeopardize centuries of mission work.

"Can he do that?" Stephen asked.

"Bishops are the ultimate power in the Anglican, or Episcopal, church. If you had attended church last Sunday, you would have heard your father read the letter from the vestry. They condemned quite openly what had happened in the churches in Puerto Rico and Panama when the Americans came."

"Dey want to keep us out of God's house," Beulah said, her voice getting louder.

Stephen, in danger of precipitating what he had intended to prevent, took refuge in silence and sipping his drink. Father Morrow saved the situation by suggesting to Beulah that the time had come for them to leave. With a baleful look, Beulah subsided.

"If you want to know what happened, Stephen, ask your father or Mark. *They* were both in church," Father Morrow said as he and Beulah departed.

When Stephen rejoined his brother to question him, Mark was not in the mood for discussion, saying he was tired and suggested that they remove the punch bowl so the hangers-on would leave.

"Aren't you supposed to go home and let Mother know how everything went? I'm staying at the town house tonight. I want to be sure that the office and the warehouse are properly protected. God knows how long the Transfer celebrations will go on with all the rum shops open. The crowd may get a little wild."

Stephen objected that he had a right to know about his father's public pronouncements in church, especially since he was volunteering his son's services to the new administration. Mark agreed to get a copy of the vestry minutes for him. "Don't say anything about it to Mother. You know she gets upset when Father starts quoting the Bible."

Stephen insisted that he was tired of delays. Mark closed his eyes and sighed before opening them, "You and the American Navy should get along just fine. Very well. The vestry agreed that the American church should be co-extensive with its Empire..."

"America?" interrupted Stephen. "America an empire?"

"Those were the terms they used. They also said it was natural that the congregation should lean toward Antigua, from which they had received all their past care. Father then observed that the West Indian church had evolved further toward the ideal of the brotherhood of man and there was no turning back now. He reminded them that when Saint Paul challenged the Roman Empire only a few in number gathered around him. After Father said that, the vestry voted that they would not change to a segregated church no matter what the jurisdiction."

"How like Father to compare himself to Saint Paul."

Mark laughed. "There are worse models. Don't take it so seriously."'

"And the United States to the Roman Empire! Why did you all vote so openly to become part of the United States if you felt that way? After all, we were quite happy being part of Denmark for two hundred years."

"How happy can you be when you're getting poorer and poorer and invasion is a threat? Not here, maybe, but in Denmark a real possibility? American rule is better than the Germans. You really have been secluded in that ivory tower up there in Boston. Didn't you read Ralph Henry's articles in the West End News, the clippings Father sent you? Didn't bother, did you?"

Stephen protested that he had examinations to study for and that he was working part-time in a law firm as well, as arranged by their father. He had little time to read the newspapers from home.

"Well, the Americans were worried about German submarines and the threat they posed to the Panama Canal or they wouldn't have wanted to purchase the Danish West Indies in the first place. I don't see why I have to repeat all of this for you. Read the local paper and listen to the talk around town instead of isolating yourself again, up there at La Grange with Mother. I know she missed you while you were away, but it's time to be getting to work."

"Well, Father seems to have arranged for that. Maybe working for the Administrator will be more interesting than I thought."

"Not what I'd choose. Rather be my own boss than saying 'Yes, sir' to a lot of meaningless orders. At least when Father tells me to do something, I understand why. But good luck to you, if that's what you want."

"I'm not sure it's what I want, but obviously that's what I'll be doing. At least until I figure out who and what I am in a place where the Americans have taken over."

"I think we all feel that way. I know I did, when I saw the flags change."

"You don't seem very concerned."

"As Father says, man has been a trader since the dawn of history, so I'm not going to worry any more than I have to. Business will get better, with the Navy here. They brought in a lot of equipment, but they'll need more. I'll just carry on as usual, same old way, helping Father in the business. You're the one he needs to cope with the changes."

CHAPTER TWO

"Good day," Stephen said to the only person visible at seven-thirty in the morning in the entrance hall of the Frederiksted Hospital. "Could I speak to the head nurse?"

"I am the head nurse, and you are? Wait a minute, I know you, you're Mr. Markham's son, the younger one, *el rubio*, the blonde one. Don't you remember me? I'm Miranda Muckle. We were in school together way back. I guess it must have been ten years ago."

"Yes, I remember," Stephen said, wondering how that awkward girl could have grown into this attractive, assured brown-skinned woman. "I remember. You were the smartest one in the class, the one who got sent to Denmark."

"I don't know how smart. Ralph Henry was a good teacher and I'm sure I studied the hardest. What can I do for you, Stephen?"

"I'm doing some work for the new American Administrator, Captain Warner..."

"I know who Captain Warner is. He's visited the hospital several times. Very inquisitive. Very thorough. But he found everything in order."

"Well, he's asked me to write up a report on the needs of the hospital. He said the head nurse would be the person to speak to."

"I see. Well, you're here early enough. And here I am. Did your father come in with you? I didn't hear his carriage?"

"I walked in from La Grange. I wanted to walk while it was still cool."

"I see."

Stephen controlled the impulse to explain that Captain Warner had asked so many questions about Frederiksted that a careful look at the once-familiar was required for any accurate report. From Fort Frederik on the northern end of town, where the sheep pastures of Estate La Grange faded into a swamp on one side and gradually assumed the shape of a street on the other, Stephen had been able to retrace the trail of his own life, each step bringing a different recollection of growing up on the western end of the island. The landmarks of his childhood-- the Fort where his birth was recorded, the Danish school he and Mark had intermittently attended, the boarded-up German consulate, the private high school, the hospital, the fish market at Miller Bay. A hazy, unfocussed, background for the daily life of one small boy on a tiny island, but a place where just a few weeks ago the political control of one colonial power had ceased to exist and another had laid its claim.

"Well, it's fortunate you were early. I must start my rounds in a few minutes."

"I wasn't the only one up so early. I saw faces looking out of the windows upstairs. I doubt that they were looking for me."

Miranda frowned. "It's that Elias. He's supposed to be opening windows and mopping floors, and instead he gets the patients all riled up. Claims he's seen German submarines and has the patients watching for more, waiting for an invasion."

"I'm sure Captain Warner would want to hear about that. How often has he seen them and at what times? I'd like to speak to Elias and the patients too."

"Elias is an ignorant man, I wouldn't believe half he says. And the patients, well, most of them don't see too well and others see things that aren't there. Since you've taken out your pencil and notebook, let me tell you about our needs."

"You've been informed, I am sure, that the request for training six student nurses made by Lieutenant Hokansen has been approved."

"Of course, one week ago, in writing. They begin training at eight o'clock this morning. But we need many more things to do the training properly. Captain Warner didn't tell you?"

"Perhaps he did mention it. I didn't know they were starting the training so soon."

"There was no reason to wait and we need nurses so badly."

"I understand you requested funds from the Colonial Council many times for training, but it was always refused."

"I know. I know. No one has to tell me that the Danes are poor. I saw it with my own eyes, but they trained me well and I'm grateful for it. But right now I can't do what is needed without more help and the supplies the Americans have promised. After all, the Navy needs this hospital too and the Americans are rich. I can give you a copy of the list I've already sent to Captain Warner."

"Please. It would save me a trip to Christiansted."

"Very well. Come along then. Lieutenant Hokansen has allowed me to select the trainees, and he has brought in an assistant to teach anatomy and physiology. It's wonderful to have all that help. These trainees are fortunate. To be trained right here."

"You didn't enjoy being sent away?"

"In a way. I always appreciated the opportunity. Your father helped, did you know that? He was one of the burghers who paid my way. That's what we called the shop owners then. Burghers. But it was far away, and cold, and dark so much of the time. People were kind, but I didn't have any real friends. I was very lonely and glad to come home. Back to the sunlight."

There was no self-pity in the soft, melodious voice. He followed her down the narrow, dark hall, freshly mopped, still damp and drying, emitting a smell of disinfectant and soap. Heeding Miranda's words of caution about slipping and breaking a leg, Stephen walked carefully, determined not to become a patient.

Six young women with expectant eyes and tense bodies clothed in blue denim uniforms waited in a small room at the end of the hall. Their backbones were pressed against the caning of the straight-backed chairs lined against the fading yellow wall. Above them the countenances of the King and Queen of Denmark hovered protectively. Stephen made a mental note to have these vestiges of royalty replaced with photographs of President Wilson and Captain Warner.

"Stand up, girls, and say hello to Mr. Stephen Markham. He has come to congratulate you for being selected for nurse's training."

"If you all do as well as Miss Miranda, the Administration will be very satisfied." The perfunctory phrase was past his lips before he recognized Alice Hansen. "Alice, how nice to see you here. You always wanted to be a nurse."

Childhood memories flashed before his eyes, silencing him with their clarity. Alice, too young to be a playmate, but frequently at Estate La Grange nonetheless, the messenger carrying the fresh leaves of the sugar apple bush her father grew and his mother brewed for her afternoon tea, pronouncing the steaming concoction "good for her health".

Alice smiled. "And you wanted to raise crabs and iguanas."

"My father had other ideas. But I'm glad I did what he wanted."

"In those days we did what our parents wanted," Miranda said. "If you'll follow me to my office, I'll give you the list for the Administrator."

Her tone had softened and Stephen noticed that the bodies of the standing girls had relaxed when he and Alice exchanged personal greetings. "You may sit down now, girls," Miranda said, "I'll be back in just a few minutes. Be ready to begin the day."

"Good luck to all of you," Stephen said. "I'll be working in Captain Warner's office as part of his staff. I'm sure he'll want to be informed of your progress. Nice to see you, Alice."

"Say hello to your mother for me."

He shook hands with the students, embarrassed by the slight curtsey each performed, though Alice's was little more than placing her right foot behind her left.

"Perhaps Dr. Hokansen could see me now," Stephen said as Miranda handed him a list of 'Urgent Needs. Frederiksted Hospital. April. 1917.' "

"His office is at the end of the hall. It's a little early for him, but he may be there. Please don't detain him for long. He has a meeting with the nurses."

Dr. Hokansen's skin was the same mottled, pale yellow of the hospital walls. But his eyes were bright and the voice strong. *Fever has colored his flesh, but not weakened his spirit,* Stephen thought. The large, battered wooden desk and the three shabby chairs, well-used and reliable, were an appropriate setting. But the paintings, two large and one small, that blazed out from the walls were unexpected. Stephen stared at them without speaking.

"Overpowering, aren't they?" Hokansen asked. "When I had them hanging behind my desk I couldn't get people to look at me. Even now, they distract my patients. But they add to my life."

"Where did you get them?"

"In Panama. From a French laborer hanging around the Canal, begging for work. I didn't want a portrait, not of this malarial face, but I did want an accurate record of the tropical plants I was using for my research, the ones with medicinal value. That's why I requested this post, to continue my research. Please sit down, Mr. Markham."

"Thank you," Stephen said, trying to remember what he had come for. "My mother is an artist, or tries to be. She hasn't been well now for a number of years. Painting means a lot to her, though it's mainly hibiscus flowers on teacups and dinner plates."

"She's not suffering from malaria, is she?"

"No, not malaria. There's no fever. Something in the blood, it seems, and she believes a local herb is helping her. In any case, she feels better when she makes a tea of it and drinks a cup each morning. Until a doctor will visit her at home and can tell what is wrong with her and can recommend some more effective treatment, she won't come near the hospital."

"Maybe she is right. Well, my official mission is to wipe out the anopheles and aedes egypti mosquitoes here as we did in Panama, get rid of malaria and yellow fever. Should be easier here. These are islands, after all. The trade winds blow all year, and there's no real wet season like we have in the Canal Zone. But we may need help in explaining to the people that we must spray everything. I hope there will be no objections, but if there are Captain Warner has assured me you will see that they are overcome."

Stephen mentioned that there would be the usual objections to something that had never been done before.

"It had never been done before in Panama either, but we did it. And because we did it, we succeeded where the French failed and the laborers we brought in--some of them from here, by the way--didn't die and that's why we, and not the French, could build the Canal."

"This is not Panama…"

"Don't waste my time with the obvious." The doctor was beginning to sound impatient and Stephen agreed that his facile observation was unnecessary, very much a lawyer's tactic. He was talking to a busy doctor, detaining him from some important task, not interviewing a witness. While Stephen tried to think of the right question, Lieutenant Hokansen continued, "I hope you will do everything you can to make our health campaign acceptable because Captain Warner has decided it must be done immediately. He also considers it a military operation, not just a health issue. I'm responsible for the health of the troops as well as the local population. Do you have any suggestions?"

"Yes. The best way is to allow the nurses, perhaps your new trainees, to explain what you want done to their friends and families, not just give a military order. The people are not used to that approach."

"These islands are hardly unfamiliar with the military. The Danish militia has been here for almost two hundred years."

"To keep order, to provide defense, not interfere in people's lives."

Stephen noted the frown of displeasure on Dr. Hokansen's face and feared a severe reprimand, perhaps a repetition of the charges often made by Ralph Henry that sexual transgression was a way of interfering in people's lives and that rape in some societies was considered a crime. But after a lengthy pause and a deep breath, the doctor finally said, "I understand you are a lawyer, Mr. Markham."

"Yes sir, I graduated this past June."

"Then you have not actually practiced law?"

"I did an internship with a very reputable law firm. And it was there I learned that one of the basic principles of law is that successful social change is best accomplished in an atmosphere of trust and confidence."

"I see. You quote the textbooks very accurately. Well, I've been practicing medicine for many years in areas where rapid change was necessary to save people's lives and that is what we intend to accomplish here. Captain Warner expects you to establish whatever atmosphere of trust and confidence that is necessary."

"But I can't do that alone!"

"Of course not. Identify your allies. Wasn't that in your textbooks? I must ask you to excuse me now. The new trainees are waiting for me. Don't forget the list Nurse Muckle gave you. I hope you will come in frequently and report your progress as we begin the eradication campaign."

"I felt like eradicating him, along with the anopheles and aedes aegypti," Stephen complained to his mother at lunch. "What a pompous ass! I never did like the military. Treating me like a schoolboy!"

Kristin Markham laughed. "It's so good to have you home again, Stephen. You always could amuse me."

"I wasn't trying to be funny."

"Of course not. Your irreverence delights me. I've gotten so tired of proper behavior. But be honest, Stephen, from that doctor's point of view you are a schoolboy, or were until recently, anyway. You must be more prudent if you want to succeed with these people. Be persistent. Since I've become ill, I've learned to live alone with my art and my flowers, but I'm still curious, you are my eyes and ears on the world. You come rushing home for lunch after telling me this morning you expected to spend the whole day in town. You drink three glasses of maubi before you say a word. Who else did you see at the hospital this morning?"

Stephen told his mother he had met Miranda Muckle, the head nurse and his old playmate, Alice Hansen, who was one of the student nurses. He felt the interview had gone well. Kristin nodded and smiled. "Yes, I know. I heard that you were at the hospital from the gardener, who knows Alice. I'm very happy for her, glad she's found something to do with her life. She's always been such a restless, ambitious child. And then you met Lieutenant Hokansen. Or is it Doctor?"

"Both. The Administrator called him 'Lieutenant' but Miranda called him 'Doctor'.

"Think I'll stick to Lieutenant. The mere word 'Doctor' is repulsive to me."

"I rather liked him at first," Stephen said. "He's obviously been ill. Yellow fever, maybe. Or malaria. His skin is yellow. He has some amazing paintings, right there in his office."

"Really? They must have been extraordinary, for you to notice them."

"There was no way you could ignore them. You'd like them, they're full of flowers. Lieutenant Hokansen said the drawing of the flowers was accurate, but they didn't look like real flowers to me. But I can still see them. Yes, they did impress me."

Kristin Markham said that as much as she would like to see the paintings nothing would drag her down to the doctor's office. "I know you, Stephen. You didn't like him for some reason. Why?"

"He started ordering me about, telling me what had to be accomplished. Immediately. Imagine! Immediately. Here, where nothing happens fast."

Kristin laughed again, touching his hand as she did so. "You never did like being told what to do. But then when you did it, whatever it was, it was done very well."

Stephen felt his anger ebbing in response to his mother's laughter and her soft, cool fingers. He noted the disappearance of the customary sadness from her face. "I told him I would need help. Than God I have you."

"I don't see what I can do. I'm really quite helpless. And you're very capable."

"I've been away so long. I don't know where to start."

"Nonsense. You've already started. Just this morning with Miranda and Alice. And then the party the other evening. Mark told me you invited Beulah, who'd been overlooked. And Ralph Henry was there. You spoke to him, didn't you?"

"Yes, of course. I know he's now considered a threat of some kind, but for me he's always my old schoolteacher."

"That's a strong bond. And now you're both lawyers. And it wasn't easy for him, Stephen. He must have studied hard, all alone, by correspondence to do well enough to pass the examinations. Just approach him as your former teacher and a fellow lawyer. Convince him you're looking after the health of the people with this eradication program. He reaches everyone through that newspaper of his. No one *wants* to get sick, you know."

"I wish you would go see Dr. Hokansen. He tells me there are new medicines…"

"I'll stick with the bush tea I learned about from Mr. Hansen, thank you. I'm careful what I eat."

"But Mother, Mr. Hansen is just a chemist at the rum factory."

His mother's only reply was to announce that she was going to rest. "I'll see you at dinner. Perhaps your father will grace us with his presence for a change, now that you've come home."

"Maybe he'll have some good ideas for me. After all, he forced me to take this job."

"That's his way. But it doesn't mean you can count on him for help. He's never around when *I* need him."

Kristin walked away from the table before Stephen could question this response. Her silver and gold hair gleamed in the sunlight coming in through the large arched window as she passed by. Stephen lingered at the table watching some peahens stroll across the front driveway, pecking at invisible bugs. He wondered if they ate mosquitoes.

"You finished, Master Stephen?" Clorinda, the serving maid, asked.

"Yes, thanks. It was very good."

Clorinda sniffed. Stephen looked up from her gnarled hands to the unlined cheeks of the still-youthful face, dark skin surrounded by a halo of white hair, a color change that had taken place in his absence. "Not much of a meal for a strong young man, cabbage soup, a little steamed fish, black bread. At least you had some decent guavaberry patty. Your mother won't touch it no more. Acts as if it's poison."

"It was delicious. Tell me, do you have a lot of mosquitoes in the kitchen?"

"Mosquitoes? Of course not. No flies, either. We have screens on the windows, right from your father's store. I keep the door shut to the back yard. Did you ever find a fly or a mosquito in your food? I should say not."

"Don't get vexed. I just wanted to know."

"I can't speak for the garden outside. None in the house."

Writing out his notes at the dining room table throughout the afternoon, Stephen found out that Clorinda was right about the flies and mosquitoes. The room was cool, shaded by the large mango tree outside the front window. A light breeze ruffled his papers, which he secured by placing salt and pepper shakers on them. A gecko, which paled whenever it intermittently paused on the white sheets of paper as it crossed and re-crossed the table, found no mosquitoes. The gecko's disapproving stare distracted Stephen, but remembering his mother's command that these small insect-consuming dragons were to be left undisturbed, he alternately stared back, then concentrated on a report he found less interesting than the gecko. His father and brother arrived at dusk.

"There you are," Cedric Markham said. "I was expecting you back in town."

"It was cool and convenient working here," Stephen answered.

"But not very professional People came in asking for you, and it was embarrassing to say I didn't know where you were."

"I walked to town and back. It was a beautiful morning."

"It's not a good idea to be seen walking in alone. People may say we don't enjoy each other's company."

"Sorry. I'll ride with you and Mark tomorrow morning."

"You're all here," Kristin said as she entered the room. "What a delightful surprise."

Kristin's hair encircled her head in a thick braid. She wore a creamy shade of white, a diaphanous extension of her pale skin. The coolness of her appearance contrasted with the warmth of her welcoming smile.

"I can't stay for dinner," Mark said. "I've been invited over to Granard and I'm taking Dr. Sampson along to meet some friends of Cousin Dee Dee's. He's pretty lonely, I think. Hasn't met any young women."

"Sampson?" Stephen asked. "Isn't that the new doctor? The one who's going to teach anatomy? He has six young nurse trainees who are anxious to meet him."

"Don't be stupid, Stephen," Mark said. "I'm talking about young ladies of his own class and color."

Stephen flushed at the rebuke. "If I recall correctly, the Granard cousins aren't exactly lily white."

"That's enough," Cedric Markham said. "You're both grown men and you're quarreling just the way you did when you were young boys. It upsets your mother. Stephen, I don't want you to make disparaging remarks alike that about your own family."

"What's disparaging about the truth?"

"It was the tone of your voice. I said, stop arguing. We all know who's socially acceptable and who isn't."

"If you're not sure, just ask your father," Kristin said. "After all, he decides. Everything. I prefer quarreling to giving orders."

"Has it occurred to you that our standards and Dr. Sampson's might be different? American law is ambiguous on racial purity," Stephen said, hoping he sounded professional and objective.

"Did you come to any decision about another carriage?" Kristin interceded.

"Are you going to buy another carriage?" Mark asked excitedly, his good humor restored. "We really need another one."

"We need more transportation, so I'm considering it," Cedric Markham said. "I'm even thinking about buying an automobile. If I accept the offer of a dealership it might be a good example to buy one myself. But perhaps I should buy a bus first, to take people back and forth to Christiansted. It should be profitable."

Mark agreed that a bus might be a good idea since most people could afford little more than a donkey cart. He also complained that both donkey carts and horses and carriages were both too slow, so he planned to ride the new stallion to Granard and invited Stephen to join him. "You can use Mother's horse. She never rides any more."

"It tires me too much" Kristin said. "A car would be nice. You're certainly welcome to my horse. Why don't you go with Mark?"

Stephen declined, pleading fatigue.

"Too much walking in the hot sun. I'll look into buying a car as soon as the shipping returns to normal. It's hurting our business, all this fuss about submarines. But the Americans will take care of that situation soon enough," Mr. Markham said.

"You see, Stephen, nothing to worry about," Kristin Markham said. "Nothing at all to worry about. Your father has said so."

CHAPTER THREE

At Stephen's insistence, all of the windows of the hospital were fitted with screens within three days. This resulted in a moderate profit for Markham and Sons, Inc. Cedric Markham refused to charge more than the usual price, even though Mark reminded him that "rush jobs" should be priced higher. Stephen, refusing to participate in the argument, was nevertheless distracted from the report he was trying to finish.

"Absolutely not," Cedric Markham said to Mark. "You know perfectly well that every one in town will know the price before the last window's screened, and so will the Navy. A small town forces one to be honest. I've told you that a hundred times."

"I wasn't suggesting dishonesty," Mark objected. "You did work the men pretty hard. A little extra for them..."

"Look ahead. If they work fast and do the job well, the Navy will have plenty of work for us, and them. That in turn will mean more work for us. More than ever before. We had better order more screen material. Greed is one of the cardinal sins. Sloth is another."

Whenever Cedric Markham introduced "religious" terminology into his arguments, his sons became otherwise occupied or quickly changed the subject. Stephen turned back to writing his report to Captain Warner noting, with satisfaction, the completion of the screening while reluctantly adding the patients' objection. Screens interfered with their view of the sea.

"They can't stick their heads out the window any more," Elias, the custodial worker and self-appointed mediator, had reported after intercepting Stephen in the hospital hallway the previous day. As Elias talked, he twisted his body around the mop handle in such a way that it appeared to be an extension of his skeleton and he could lean on it for support. "They can't see if the submarines are coming."

"Who has actually seen a submarine?" Stephen asked, not for the first time.

"A lot of ém. Dey're 'fraid to say so. It vexes Nurse Muckle, and when she vexed at you, she won't give you no pain medicine."

Miranda laughed at the criticism when Stephen repeated it to her. "Such nonsense. The doctor prescribes the dosage. I just administer it. Sometimes he may cut back a little when they start seeing things that aren't there. Elias is lazy and a liar as well. Makes up all kinds of stories to get attention. I would like to fire him, but he's one of Ralph Henry's godchildren and I said I would give him a chance. Go ask Ralph what kind of a man Elias is."

Stephen remembered to ask about Elias when he went to the newspaper office to see his former teacher, isolated from outside interference by inside clutter and the noise of the printing press. Despite his rolled-up shirt sleeves and loosened tie, Ralph Henry greeted Stephen with formality and turned off the machinery so they could hear each other speak.

"Good-day, Mister Stephen. Nice of you to pay me a visit."

"I hope I'm not disturbing you."

"Not at all. Not at all. Always a pleasure to talk with a colleague. What can I do for you?"

Stephen repeated Nurse Muckle's warning about Elias and asked Ralph Henry's opinion about the reliability of Elias's reports. "I'm afraid she's right. He likes attention, does Elias. And Miranda, well, if you can't trust a nurse, who can you trust? As long as she's there, we can be reasonably sure that the white doctors don't poison us. We need more like her in our hospital. "

"I agree. So does the Administrator. That is why the government is proceeding with the nurses' training," Stephen said. He glanced through the dusty window at the three barefoot young boys breaking off the smaller twig-like branches from the genip tree in the backyard. They were eating the fruit as fast as they picked it, tearing at the brittle skin to reveal the pulp, their teeth bared like carnivorous animals. "Are you troubled much by mosquitoes?"

Ralph Henry smiled. "So that's why Captain Warner sent you here."

"Well, as a matter of fact..."

"So the representative of the greatest power on earth wants a favor from a poor black man. Now I wonder what it could be. I'm printing the truth in my newspaper, you know, and the truth is that when the Americans come, racial discrimination is not far behind. I can prove every word I've printed about what the American Navy did in Panama and Puerto Rico. Segregating the churches. That's going pretty far, don't you think? Contradicting the word of God."

Stephen, remembering a courtroom maneuver used to distract and avoid, walked over closer to the window and stared out. "The mosquito eradication campaign saved thousands of lives in Panama and Puerto Rico, particularly those of young children."

Ralph Henry's derisive laugh did not affect the serious tone of his voice. "All right, Stephen. I'm not stupid. If the Americans have something good to give, I'll take it. That doesn't mean I'll stop fighting for the rights of my people."

"In order to be effective, eradication must be complete. No one, absolutely no one, can leave water standing around. That includes seedlings in kerosene tins and the water caught in rain barrels. This means changes in the way the people live but..."

"Just save me the trouble and send me a written copy of what you want published. But only about mosquitoes. I'm not printing any ordinances or public notices unless you check with me first about the contents."

Stephen thanked Ralph Henry formally for his cooperation saying he would let Captain Warner know immediately.

"Forget the 'Mr. Henry'. We're not teacher and student any more. We're equals now, according to law. That's right, isn't it? And I am not by nature an agreeable person, not at all. Too much struggle all my life. So just let Captain Warner know I'll go along with his public health measures, but that's as far as I will go."

As Stephen turned to leave, Ralph Henry continued, "Say hello to your father for me. Tell him I'm going to write an editorial on the stand he took at St. Paul's church." Stifling his curiosity, Stephen left without asking what his father had done, annoyed that in a community where everyone felt he had the right to know what everyone else was doing, he knew so little. Stephen walked directly to his father's office when he reached the hardware store.

"So he's doing an editorial on me," Cedric Markham said when Stephen told him what Ralph Henry had said. "I'm not sure that's a good idea. No point in making an issue of it. It only concerns our parishioners, after all."

"Do you mind telling me what 'it' is?" Stephen asked impatiently.

"No, I don't mind, though you'd know if you went to church on Sundays like the rest of us. We had to tear down the upstairs gallery at St. Paul's. It was full of termites and ready to collapse. I suggested, actually insisted, that it not be rebuilt and the tradition of having the natives sit up there be completely abandoned. Now we all sit together downstairs, no reserved pews."

"And everyone agreed?"

"They did have much choice, since I was the one they expected donate the new gallery. I offered to repair the belfry instead. That was in pretty bad shape too."

"But Ralph Henry says it is Navy policy to segregate the churches."

"Does he? I guess I'd better read his editorial. I must get down to the pier. Perhaps you'll come to church with Mark and me on Sunday."

Stephen saw no reason to include any reference to the church repairs in his weekly report to Captain Warner, which he delivered to Christiansted before noon on Friday mornings. His first reports had been criticized as being "too abstract". He hoped these would meet with approval.

"I want to know what's going on and feel I've been there," Captain Warner said. "Your reports are getting better but give me details, specifics. Visit the hospital every day if necessary. Keep after Ralph Henry. I'll judge what's important and what isn't. I simply don't have the time to be going back and forth to Frederiksted." Then as an afterthought he added, "Perhaps you could stay to lunch. My wife has expressed a desire to meet you. We have a son about your age, you know. A little younger. Just graduated from the Naval Academy at Annapolis."

In contrast to his earlier interview with Captain Warner, little response and few explanations were required of Stephen during the luncheon. The dark-haired, thin-faced Mrs. Warner lost her pallor as she chattered incessantly, her face turning pink as she did so. By the end of the meal, a sunburn red crept up into her cheeks and her dark eyes gleamed brightly.

"So warm here. As bad as Panama. I thought that after all those years of living in a country that was practically a jungle we deserved to be sent back to civilization or posted in Washington. We would have been near my son. But no. More tropics. More heat."

Stephen later described the luncheon to his curious mother as an exercise in listening to complaints. "I didn't really know what this job would be like but I didn't know it would include that. At least Mrs. Warner has a soft, southern voice. She didn't ask any personal questions, just complained about the Navy, the heat, and Saint Croix. The most important thing in her life is her son. The food was good, and so was the sherry served before lunch."

"What's wrong with Cruzan rum? Haven't these people heard of cocktails? And they call us provincial! I get so tired of hearing the Americans find fault with our islands. It's just another way of telling us how superior they are. But forget these petty officials, they aren't important. Tell me about Government House. How did it look? In my day it was so well cared for."

"Your day isn't exactly over, Mother. Government House looks the way I remember it, full of highly polished antiques the Danes left behind. I can't say I care much for those floor-length gilt mirrors, kind of ridiculous for some little island in the Caribbean to attempt to copy Versailles. Fortunately, we had lunch on the balcony overlooking the interior patio. The big, old mahogany trees haven't moved an inch in two hundred years. Nothing pretentious about *them.*"

"Now who's being critical? Don't forget you were born here and we all have our dreams and fantasies, even those of us who live on little islands. There are mahogany trees all over the island, but only one Government House with a ball-room and floor-length, gilded mirrors. When all of Europe wanted sugar, that ballroom wasn't ridiculous and we could afford a few fantasies."

"And a few slaves?"

"I'm tired of arguing about that. We weren't here then, and there's no excuse for not maintaining a beautiful build-ing. Maybe you're not old enough to feel re-invigorated by beauty, but that's the effect it has on me. That's why I grow hibiscus and try to paint. The need for beauty." Kristin Markham paused and Stephen could think of no suitable reply at the moment. The right words would come later perhaps, as he was falling asleep, some phrase to show he understood would come unbidden to his mind. He liked to evoke his mother's often odd observations, replay them in his mind, savor them even though he knew the words would be forgot-ten by morning.

"What does Mrs. Warner look like?" Kristin Markham continued. "Is she a good-looking woman? I haven't gone to any of the tea-parties for her. Women who talk all the time when they get someone who must listen are usually lonely. I've heard she drinks."

"However in the world did you hear something like that?"

"I'm not entirely cut off from the world, you know. I have a few people who visit me. I'm not ashamed to admit that we gossip. More fun than complaining."

Stephen said he saw no indication of drinking beyond a sherry before lunch. The real luxury was very cool water served with lunch, indicating that there must be ice stored somewhere in the cellars of Government House. "I think people would consider Mrs. Warner a good-looking woman. She wore a pretty dress, blue, I think. But you're right, I got tired of the complaining. Unpleasant to be around for very long."

"I didn't say she drank publicly. She's a brandy sipper. Drinks alone while she smokes a cigarette. I bet she doesn't smoke in public either."

"That kind of information comes from the servants. I'm surprised at you, gossiping with the help."

"They know everything. There's always some truth in gossip. I never did trust soft-voiced women. I like women who speak their minds, loud and clear."

"Well, Saint Croix has plenty of those. Men too. Captain Warner didn't mention it, but I doubt that he would have approved of the stand Father took about eliminating the balcony in the Anglican Church."

"It wasn't so much really. No one's been sitting in that balcony for months. It was unsafe. Everyone said so, anyway. No one wants the laborers and the servants to be injured. It's all right for me to lie around doing nothing most of the time, but if Clorinda was hurt no one would get a decent meal around here. There's one thing about your father - I know it, you know it, and Captain Warner had better learn it, --don't argue with your father about the church. In most ways, he's a reasonable man, but not about that. Just like *his* father."

Stephen noted that neither he nor Mark had never been much concerned with church matters, but Kristin Markham refused to be distracted from her reminiscing. "Grandpa Markham ran his business with his Bible on his desk. I've seen him put his hand on it and make a short prayer before he announced a business decision. I guess it worked. He built up a good business. Your father was just a child when they came here from Connecticut and his father brought him up the same way he ran his business, by the Bible. Neither one of them had any success in changing me. They never said so, but I'm sure they both thought all Europeans are to some degree atheistic and decadent. They couldn't say anything though, because I had a clergyman grandfather of my own and could sing hymns along with the best of them. Before I got sick, anyway."

Stephen recalled the well-worn Bible on his father's desk, a memento of the clergymen ancestors on both sides of his family. "I never heard that story before," he said.

"Well, you're older now and there are some things you should understand about your father when I'm not around any more."

"Please don't talk that way."

"Who knows, prayer *may* help me get better. Which reminds me, Easter is this Sunday. I'd better rest up for that. I like the Easter music at the Lutheran church."

Stephen immediately offered to accompany his mother. There would be no escaping church on Easter and he preferred his mother's company to that of his father and brother. He admitted to himself it was a way of seeing Alice Hansen again and was thus rewarded when he had the opportunity to approach her after the service as churchgoers stood around talking to friends. His mother was pulled aside by a Danish-speaking woman she seemed happy to see, and Alice was standing alone, apparently waiting for her parents who were part of the choir.

"It's nice to have a chance to talk to you for a minute," Stephen said. "You're always running somewhere when I go to the hospital to check on the training."

"God help us if we don't walk fast," Alice said. "Miss Muckle says you don't walk slowly when a patient really needs something. The way she watches us! The only time we get to sit down is when we have a class."

"The trainees are all doing well, she tells me. I've passed that information on to the Administrator."

"I can't wait until we finish. My daddy says he'll send me to New York to continue my training if I do well."

"You'll be leaving?" Stephen was surprised at the pang of disappointment he felt.

"Oh, I truly hope so. I want to see New York. Now that we're all going to become American citizens, it's easier to travel there. Your mother looks well. I haven't seen much of her now that she's growing her own bush tea. She missed you terribly while you were away. It's good that you're back."

"Here comes Mother now. She's feeling well today, I think," Stephen said as his mother joined them, smiling warming at Alice.

"Happy Easter. How pretty you look! And what a lovely dress," Kristin Markham said.

"My mother made it. She complains that I never wear decent clothes anymore, just uniforms."

"Such a talented woman, your mother," Kristin said. "I never could sew. It's one of the few things I envy about these women from America. They can buy clothes, ready-made, in a store. But what I really admire about your mother is how beautifully she plays the organ. Bach isn't easy, you know. I had to take piano lessons for years when I was a girl, and I never could play Bach properly."

"I never wanted to. I preferred playing with frogs and lizards, like Stephen. Mother was disappointed, said I was behaving like a proper pickaninny with my bare feet in the mud. But my father didn't mind. Said I might become a scientist or a chemist like him."

"And work at the rum factory?"

"I think a pharmacy was what he had in mind."

"Tell your father I enjoyed the choir. Martin Luther could certainly write powerful hymns. 'A Mighty Fortress is Our God'. When I hear that strong voice of your father's-- he sings with such conviction, I can almost believe that God is a fortress. In any case, I know my husband does. Stephen, we had better leave. I'm sorry now that I said I would go to Granard for lunch, but I promised. Good-bye, Alice. I miss your visits."

"Keep well, Mrs. Markham. Perhaps you'll visit the hospital some time."

"Not if I can help it. Have a nice Easter."

The carriage ride to Granard was tiring, particularly since they had to stop and pick up Mark and Mr. Markham at the Anglican Church. It was obvious that Kristin Markham was exhausted before the first event in the Easter ritual, a polo game, began. The well-tended field was bordered on the south by a dirt road along the shore, the driveway to the Plantation House and cane fields on the other two sides. As the spectators watched the male Granard cousins play polo, they could also evaluate the condition of the crop that made the game possible.

The proficient players within the family alternated at making up a team, which challenged "outsiders", non-siblings, but usually close relatives. Only the most elite, the "four families", a term invented by Ralph Henry with intended irony but accepted with some sense of pride by the so-described, were permanent members of the teams. Relatives and guests were occasionally invited to play if they were good enough horsemen. Mark was a Sunday regular with the challenging team, a group he was responsible for recruiting. Stephen consistently begged off, preferring solitary swimming or occasionally sailing if he could find a suitable companion.

But he could not escape the family ritual at Easter, albeit in the minor role of spectator. He was grateful that this Easter Sunday a sudden, torrential shower intervened to make the game impossible. Much as they would have enjoyed polo, planters could not curse a blessing.

Stephen doubly welcomed a somnolent Sunday after an exhausting week negotiating between Captain Warner and Ralph Henry as to the most effective method of dealing with a new problem that had recently cropped up. He found a quiet corner of the balcony to meditate on the touchy issue. Many recalcitrant citizens of Frederksted did not want "dem militiamen in de yard killin'de plants" and Stephen had been placed in the ridiculous position of being defense lawyer for a future gardenia bush by retrieving the rusted can holding a cutting, which a man spraying had overturned and then kicked aside. Moments later he had been forced to assume the role of prosecutor, refuting the arguments of some old ladies convinced that spray reduced or destroyed entirely the potency of their medicinal herbs.

Away from the fray on a festive Sunday, Stephen looked around at the various plants which rimmed the balcony of the Granard plantation house. They seemed inoffensive enough, reds, purples and pinks alternating among the glistening dark green leaves, luxuriating in the fresh moisture blowing in. No reminders of a potential military invasion disturbed this floral display. Along the balcony, which extended around all four sides of the house, the guests relaxed contentedly in cane-backed chairs, pushed back beyond the reach of the rain.

"A great Easter party, despite the weather," Mark said as he joined Stephen. "Everyone is here. Cousin Dee Dee never looked more beautiful. She's absolutely radiant. Lieutenant Sampson is really smitten with her. I'm glad I persuaded him to come."

The Markhams, the Atwaters, the MacFarlands, the Lorings,--the "four families" of Saint Croix.--they were all there, eating, drinking, gossiping, looking as well fed and serene as their plants. Polo was a diversion, a statement of ability and privilege, a chance to perform before a friendly, appreciative audience, but rain at Easter time was a good omen, especially after the long drought that usually occurred during the Lenten season. Rain was the life-blood of an island without rivers and the planters compensated for their disappointment at missing polo by calculating added profits as the raindrops fell. The handsome young naval officer so obviously fascinated by Dee Dee Macfarland, the only female among the Granard cousins, provided a ripple that traversed this sea of complaency.

"Is Lily Loring that girl with Dee Dee? She's grown up a lot," Stephen said.

"Grown up fat. Ate too much during that year in Denmark. That's a Danish friend with her. She's quite pretty. Can't hold a candle to Dee Dee, but then who can? But don't forget the eleventh commandment, no more intermarriage between cousins."

Mark went off in the direction of the young women. Stephen looked around for his mother, hoping she was ready to leave. Rain meant water gathering in kerosene cans, gutters and rain barrels. Rain meant mosquitoes, illness, the hospital, doctors, --and nurses. He pictured Alice Hansen in her pretty Easter dress, probably back in uniform by now, possibly at work. He felt useless, out of place at Granard and admitted to himself that he felt more comfortable talking with Captain Warner, or even Ralph Henry, to chatting idly with his relatives about rain or crops or polo.

CHAPTER FOUR

Miranda Muckle suggested to Stephen that an additional physician be called, in order to help with the supervision of the mosquito sprayings. His presence, she said, would probably make the program more acceptable to the local residents. "Dr. Ramlov's a retired Danish doctor. Everybody knows and respects him."

"Retired from what?"

Miranda explained that Dr. Ramlov was a physician sent by the Danish government to serve as a doctor and pharmacist to the Danish garrison. He had the added responsibilities of being in charge when they opened a clinic in Frederiksted and had arranged for the training of our first local nurses by the Danish Sisters. "That's what the Danes called the nurses, remember? He stayed on here when he retired. He told me he had no family left in Denmark and all his friends were here. He could live better off here on his pension. The people listen to and respect him."

Captain Warner approved the suggestion when Stephen passed it on, but insisted that Dr. Ramlov be paid. "Tell Lieutenant Hokansen to determine what a decent stipend should be and I'll sign the necessary approval. I know what doctors in the tropics have to go through and I doubt if he gets much of a pension. Not everyone's as generous as the

Americans. Besides, I don't trust civilian volunteers. They don't take orders well."

Stephen planned to follow the plan for spraying given to him by Lieutenant Hokansen, a carefully annotated grid of both Frederiksted and Christiansted as well as outlying districts. To the section describing how gutters along the roofs of the houses should be cleaned and cleared of obstructions and how water barrels and potted plants should be carefully inspected, Stephen, to avoid the attacks of easily offended grandmothers, attached a directive that any seedlings found in small cans should be drained and carefully repositioned in the spot where they were found.

He dutifully observed the first spraying at a small white house with gingerbread trim over the balcony, the first of similar shorefront dwellings along Strand Street. The busy thoroughfare ran north to south beside the sea, from the fish market at the southern end to the Fort on the north, lined with shops and warehouses on the land side and with multiple small landing docks along the beach, separating while simultaneously connecting both home and work, Frederiksted with the world.

The majority of the houses were small, with hibiscus and bougainvillea halfway concealing streetside balconies and larger backyards where carefully nurtured provisions were grown. Halfway down the street were two much larger and more imposing structures, one formerly occupied by the Danish gendarmes and the other by the defunct German Consulate, both now empty and forlorn, seemingly awaiting new occupants. Spraying around these would present no problem. Stephen decided, somewhat reluctantly, it was probably better to confront whatever objections might arise from the occupants of the smaller houses on this initial visit while Dr. Ramlov was accompanying him.

The scowling owner of the first house, his wife, and two small children clinging and peeking from behind her madras skirt, watched the four uniformed men cover the plants on the front balcony with a smelly, oily substance. Then the spraying crew plodded silently into the rear yard and over-turned small kerosene cans filled with brown rust-filled water. Dr. Ramlov issued some warnings. "Careful where you step. The chickens run loose in here and please don't spray any of them, for God's sake. Don't throw away the water in the receptacles just any place; pour it onto their herbs, around the base, not on the leaves. We can't have people eating kerosene and pyrethrum. Leave the large rain-barrel by the drainage spout, just spray the surface to kill the larvae. Any plants in the house, Samuel?" he asked the man who followed him in sullen silence.

"All on de balcony. De need sun. Need water too."

"Don't worry, Samuel," Dr. Ramlov said. "Make sure you only take the water from the bottom of the barrel and be sure to boil it if you're going to use if for drinking or cooking." He put his hand on the man's shoulder and Samuel looked less sullen. "I brought you into this world and I wish you to stay here for a good while. Can't have your children getting the fever, either. You're a smart man. You're doing what's right for yourself and your family. When the Navy is finished there'll be no more malaria or fever on this island."

The spraying of Strand Street, including the two large empty residences, was completed before noon. When the spraying crew ran out of fluid, Dr. Ramlov's advised stopping for the day. "We've been here since seven o'clock. None of us should be breathing too much of that stuff," Dr. Ramlov said.

"One of the reasons I've always loved the Indies is because of the fresh, pure air and yet here I am helping you to contaminate it. I'm not complaining, mind you. I know this spraying is a good thing. I've seen too many babies die of fever and too many able-bodied men grow weak from malaria. I'll be more than happy to supervise the spraying for you. To witness the mosquitoes eradicated, the end of fever in the Danish West Indies--sorry, American Virgin Islands-- that would be a great day for any physician. I'm not very busy these days. Just visit a few old patients who don't have the sense to go to a younger doctor. "

"Captain Warner wants the spraying completed as quickly as possible."

"It will be just as efficient to refill the tanks this afternoon and be ready for an early start tomorrow morning. You asked for help and advice. I'm giving it."

Stephen, relaxing now that the day's task had been completed without trouble from the residents, took a more thorough look at the doctor who had been so helpful, wondering how this skinny old man could wear, in the tropical heat, a frock coat over a high-collared shirt and black tie. There was something familiar about the bright blue eyes, the beak-like nose and the tan wrinkled skin. "I remember you now, Dr. Ramlov," he said. "You used to visit my mother."

"That's right. We're old friends. Lillian Loring, your mother and I used to ride together. That stopped when Lillian died so suddenly and your mother fell ill. I was their doctor and yet I couldn't help either one of my dear friends. We still haven't found anything better than bush tea to treat the sugar disease. She's a brave woman, your mother. I've heard she sticks to her diet, no sweets and plenty of oatmeal. No rum. Definitely no rum. I told her that. Too bad. We used to have some good laughs over rum swizzles when we were young and your parents held parties at La Grange."

"You were part of the group that used to sit around and tell stories about Denmark. I remember."

"Yes, it was so pleasant to reminisce about a place you really never wanted to see again. Last time I went back home for a short visit I had to stay longer than planned, right into the winter. Nothing but constant cold and darkness. I've lived in the sun too long to ever desire put up with that again. Well, give your mother my regards. I truly wish she welcomed visitors."

"She tires very easily."

"Yes, yes. I'm sure she does. She needs her rest and quiet. Don't forget to tell the Administrator everything I mentioned to you earlier, most importantly the dam. You wrote them all down, didn't you? Thank goodness. Don't let folks forget what we Danes built. We tried, you know. You Americans! Think no one else ever did anything worthwhile. I so miss working. I'll consider it my pleasure to keep my eye on the spraying crew for you."

Stephen mentioned the items on Dr. Ramlov's list to Captain Warner hesitantly and was surprised by the Administrator's enthusiasm.

"So there really is an old dam up in the hills. I've heard it mentioned and meant to look into it. And an aqueduct too, you say."

"It may be nothing more than ruins, sir. The Danes built it when sugar was thriving and Frederiksted was a busy port. That was quite a while ago."

"It's obvious you don't know much about dams and aqueducts. They're built to last for centuries. Glad you called my attention to it. It's just what we need, a good water supply."

"Actually, it was Dr. Ramlov who…"

"I don't care how you found out about it, it's important, the kind of thing I want and need to know. I've been through this before. God knows we had plenty of rain in Panama, but we were always in need of safe water. You need good dams and aqueducts for that. I have had some of my men mapping those catchments you find on the hillsides around the island, but they are not enough. Not for our troops."

"And the people, sir. Not all of them have cisterns. If they do, they're small or simply rain barrels that breed mosquitoes."

"Of course, of course. Do you think I'm some sort of unfeeling monster? I may have some reservations about the capacities of the local people, but it's good military strategy to keep them healthy and satisfied. If you ask people to dump all the rainwater they've been hoarding in old kerosene cans, you've got to come up with a decent replacement supply. I've been telling you, and I hope you've been getting across to Ralph Henry, the Navy is concerned with the health of *all* the people. Now get me the exact location of the dam. Visit it yourself. Draw me a good, simple map. Nothing complicated. Something my engineers can follow. Right away."

Mark was no help when Stephen asked for directions. "Northside Dam? There's an old path, up Mahogany Road, about a mile or two, past the Hansen place. You can find it if you look hard enough. We used to ride up there when we were kids. Don't you remember the way?

"Could we ride up there this evening after work? I don't want to waste a whole day wandering around looking for it."

"Not a chance. I'm going to play tennis with George. George Sampson, the new doctor. He's a great guy and a good tennis player. Come with us. We have a standing date every afternoon at the tennis club after work. He joins me and we ride up to the club at Beeston Hill. The girls are taking lessons and we meet them there. They watch us play singles, sometimes join us for doubles, afterwards George sees them home. He lives nearby. That's how he can get the official hospital car."

"What girls?"

"You sound just like Mother. Lily Loring. Cousin Lily. And her house guest from Denmark, Karen Viborg. And Dee Dee, of course. George is getting serious about her, I think. And Karen's going to stay on a while. I talked her into it. So, as you can see, we're all having a good time. You could be having fun too, if you hung out with the right people more. Cousin Lily's always asking about you. They all say you're not the same since you went away to college and law school. Cold and distant, no fun any more. Lily's not a real cousin you know. Her mother was a close friend of Mother's."

"Now *you* sound like Mother. Never mind. I'll find the damned Northside Dam."

Stephen's search was delayed by the holiday weekend and the Easter Monday fracas, the term Miranda used when she sent Elias to summon Stephen to the hospital at six in the morning. The Puerto Ricans had already been there, she said, protesting the (what Puerto Ricans?)invasion of their homes and property while they were absent.

"Where have you been?" Miranda demanded. "You know that the Puerto Ricans all go to the beach on Good Friday. Camp out until Sunday, sometimes until Monday."

"No, I don't know."

"The Navy spraying team should never have gone into their homes when they weren't there."

"Dr. Ramlov said he would take care of the spraying. You assured me he was reliable. Why didn't he stop them?"

"He was at the beach, of course. It was Easter Saturday. He encourages people to go swimming. Now almost as many natives go to the beach as Puerto Ricans. Where have you been all weekend?"

"I went sailing on Good Friday. Now that you mention it, the beaches were full of people, taking sea baths. Saturday I did a little exploring, trying to find a path up to Northside Dam. Never did find it. On Easter I went to church and then to Estate Granard. It rained almost the whole day, anyway."

"Well, you have to cancel the spraying this morning. Easter Monday is a holiday. Half the town is camped out at the East End beaches, and the other half has been in here complaining."

"I can't change Captain Warner's orders. He feels we have too many holidays anyway. If Saturday hadn't been part of the holiday, we would have sprayed then. I'll ask them to do behind Father's warehouse and our town house, and we can do the lot behind the hospital again, and the cemetery. Please help me out with this, Miranda. I shouldn't have left the spraying in Dr. Ramlov's hands. But he seemed so trustworthy and reliable."

Miranda protested that Dr. Ramlov was both trustworthy and reliable and any mistake had been Stephen's. She agreed that the best plan was to change the route of the spraying, saying she would explain the situation to Dr. Hokansen if Stephen made the schedule changes.

Feeling he had weathered the crisis well, Stephen was quite unprepared for the forcefulness of Captain Warner's reprimand when he went up to Christiansted to explain what had happened. "I have just received word from Washington that war against Germany has been officially declared and you inform me that most of the inhabitants of Saint Croix are at the beach!"

"It's a local holiday. Good Friday through Easter Monday. I forgot it myself. No one reminded me."

"Don't you and your family talk to each other?"

"My father observes all the religious holidays, some we don't even know about. Mark carries on the business for him. I guess he just assumed that I would remember."

"Well then, get someone else to remind you. Our warships are being sunk, Germany's trying to set up an alliance with Mexico, a German spy ring has been operating in Washington, and here, where we're supposed to be protecting the Canal, everyone goes to the beach. If you can't get Ralph Henry to write something forceful about the war threat, then do it yourself and get him to publish it. And get going with that damn Northside Dam thing. I need a good water source. And Washington wants another report on the nurse training program before they release more funds."

Stephen was not invited to stay to luncheon that day so returned earlier than usual to Frederiksted. He ran into Alice Hansen coming out of the hospital. She looked exhausted and without hesitation Stephen offered her a lift home.

"Oh, yes. Thanks, Stephen. It's the first time I've had night duty and I'm pretty tired. Elias came in last night and told the patients that war had been declared and after that we couldn't get them to sleep. They were totally convinced an invasion was coming and wanted to watch for submarines."

"How did Elias know war had been declared? I only heard it myself from the Administrator this morning."

"Well, Ralph Henry knew and got Elias to help him set the newsprint for a special edition. Have you seen the paper?"

"No. I just got back from Christiansted. I was reprimanded because I forgot about the long Easter weekend holidays. The Puerto Ricans are angry because their homes were sprayed while they were camped out at the beach. And I'm supposed to locate the Northside Dam and I've forgotten how to get there."

Alice laughed. "You've forgotten a lot."

"I'm beginning to regret I agreed to work for the Administrator. I'm not equipped to fulfill his expectations. I'd be better off building my own law practice."

"Don't worry. You'll be on your own someday. When this war is over, we'll get rid of the Navy."

"What makes you think that?"

"People are talking about it. It won't happen for a while. In the meantime I'm going to take advantage of what the Americans have to offer. I'm going to travel to America to continue my training. Hopefully before they work me to death down here. Give me a ride home every day and I'll remind you about the holidays and local customs. And I'll even show you a shortcut to Northside Dam."

"I wish I could, but I don't always get the carriage. For the most part on Fridays. Lucky for us, Father was in church today, so he didn't need it. I don't often get back this early. This job is very inconvenient."

"And now that I'm doing probationary work", Alice said, "my hours change all the time. Oh well, it will only be for a few more months."

"How is the training program doing?"

"Pretty well, I think. But you'd be better off to talk to Miss Muckle about that. Anything we say she's likely to call 'gossip'. I'm so sick of this small town stuff. I can't wait to get to New York. There's bound to be more freedom to do and say what I please when and where I wish to say it. After all it is a big city."

"It's a big city, all right."

"You know New York?"

"Not well. Not as well as Boston. Big cities can be lonely though."

"Well, I won't be alone. My brother's there. He's a pharmacist and so is his wife. They have a little pharmacy in Harlem and I can stay with them while I finish my training at Harlem hospital. I want to be registered nurse, that way I can work anywhere. Of course, Daddy wants me to come back home. We'll see."

Once they came within the vicinity of the Hansen house Alice asked to be let off at the driveway. "If Mommy hears the carriage she'll come running out. She'll raise a big fuss when she sees that someone drove me home. Treats me like a child."

"But she knows me. All my life. I'm not a stranger, like Dr. Sampson. Does he drive you home often?"

Alice shrugged. "Who told you he drove me home? Oh, I know. It must have been Miranda Muckle. I was tired, like I was today, and he offered me a ride. I don't feel like questions and explanations when I get home. I study hard and work hard and I'm not stupid enough to fall for any sweet talk from friend or stranger. Dr. Sampson just wants to know things about life on the island and he's interested in everything. I need sleep, not arguments from my mother. I'd appreciate a ride, if you happen to pass by when I get off work. Let me know when you want to go to Northside Dam. I know how to get there. I'll take you if they ever give me a day off."

Stephen lingered to watch as she walked down the dirt driveway. Alice half-turned her body to wave goodbye. An island girl, all grown up, Stephen thought. Waves as gracefully as she walks.

Early the next morning Stephen sought out Miranda Muckle and found her uncharacteristically willing to take time off from her duties to answer questions about the nurses' training. He told her that Captain Warner needed an updated report to be sent to Washington to justify more funding.

"Well, you can say we've adhered to the schedule well. The new laboratory is finished and the class material has been covered. We don't take any holidays. I've scheduled the time-off rotation for the trainees so the patients are not left without care. Dr. Sampson is very strict about punctuality and the girls don't seem to mind when *he* gives the orders. After all he is very handsome. They've even gone through post-mortem examinations without complaint. We always had plenty when I was being trained. Complaints, I mean."

Stephen had difficulty in imagining Alice at a post-mortem, all that youth and energy observing the dissection of death. Miranda Muckle interrupted his thoughts by inviting him to accompany her to inspect some of the changes. In his notebook Stephen dutifully described the garish, brightly colored charts of internal organs, nerves and muscles now decorating the classroom where Dr. Sampson taught anatomy and physiology, the expansion of the laboratory where Dr. Hokansen expounded on public health procedures, the aseptic operating room and the cool thick-walled morgue. "I teach, too," Miranda informed him. "Dr. Hokansen has made me Instructor of the Nursing Arts. That includes most of the gynecology and obstetrics. I'm a licensed midwife, you know. Both doctors say I've been very well trained. I've had a lot of practice delivering babies. For a long time it was just Dr., Ramlov and me who took care of the mothers and babies. "

"And all the trainees are doing well?"

"Very well. Very well. We're having no trouble with *them*."

"Who is giving you trouble?"

"It's that Elias. He's a stupid, ignorant…man."

She just caught herself in time, Stephen thought. *He could feel her bite back the word "nigger."*

"What's he done now?"

"He's doing everything he can to be spiteful. Loosening the screens when he cleans, so a few mosquitoes do get in after all. Shutting the blinds on the shutters tight, so that no air gets in. Dr. Hokansen's says that fresh air at night is very important. We're extremely busy and Elias is so hard to watch. He's everywhere, you know. Cleaning this, fixing that. And now he's started going around unfixing things."

"Couldn't you just retire him. He's getting pretty old. He must have children to take care of him."

"At least twelve. We tried to get him to retire once. He said he would like to. We had a little party for him, gave him a new shirt, his friends in the scratchy band played some music, and he insisted on dancing with the nurses, even me. He came into my office the day before the party to inform me that he expected to dance with me, since he was retiring. I thought it would be well worth while to be rid of him, particularly since he was all cleaned up for the occasion and was a good dancer. Well, he had his party, his presents, and his rum…and the next day he showed up for work as usual. Been here ever since, doing what he does. Retirement, for him, meant having a party. Don't laugh."

"Well, if you can't fire him, nobody can. Everyone's afraid of you."

"Who told you that? No, don't tell me, I don't want to know. I have to be strict. Our young people would spend all their time laughing and dancing, getting nowhere, if we let them. Elias is useful sometimes. Does little errands for us. Gets me fresh bread from the bake shop as it comes out of the oven. Lets us know when the red snapper comes in to the fish market so we can get some before it's all gone. But I'm afraid that one of these days he's going to cross Dr. Sampson."

"According to my brother, he's an easy-going sort."

"Not here at the hospital. Strict as he can be, particularly with the nurses. Keeps his distance. Though that's just as well."

"What do you mean? You said the nurses presented no discipline problems?"

"Not as far as their daily work is concerned. They take orders very well. I feel responsible for their other behavior as well. Dr. Sampson is a handsome young man, and he's different from the Danes. He walks and talks so free and easy, and with that soft voice of his. They're young women, proud of themselves, and what they're doing, and I, God help me, I've encouraged them to think that way. To believe they're just as good as anybody else, maybe better. Maybe you won't understand all this, spent so much time in America, but a lot of us native women think the old way, that the best and easiest way to get ahead is to get yourself a white man. I wouldn't talk this way if I didn't care so much about the training program. Good nurses make good wives and mothers. Respectable women. We don't have to use men. Or let men use us."

"That hasn't always been the case," Stephen said defensively.

"Almost always."

Stephen had no desire to argue with Miranda. They were both aware of the West Indian tradition, that the children of European fathers and local women were usually recognized as legal offspring. Sometimes the unions were legitimized by marriage, as was the case for both sets of Alice Hansen's grandparents. The Hansen's La Grange plantation, a merger of properties inherited from Danish forefathers, was almost as large as Granard, where the same thing had occurred two generations earlier. It had not previously occurred to Stephen that such island mores and traditions could complicate the long-range public health program being administered by naval officers from Virginia.

"Should I put all this in my report to the Administrator?" Stephen asked. He wanted to lighten Miranda's mood, restore her to her usual imperturbability.

"Don't joke. It's just that with the Americans, well with the idea that everyone is, or should be, equal, perhaps these girls expect too much. Things are changing very fast."

"Dr. Sampson seemed quite smitten with my cousin Dee Dee at Granard at Easter."

"Well, I'm sure the nurses won't be happy to hear that, but I am." Miranda sighed. "I still worry about that Elias. He's sure to get himself in trouble, getting so cocky, says Ralph Henry tells him he has the same rights as anyone else."

"These Navy men know how to deal with that. They're concerned with rank and discipline, not equality. They can be very tough when necessary."

"Please God you're right. But if the Navy disciplines Elias, he'll go running to Ralph Henry and get him all worked up.

Don't say anything at the moment. I'll try to figure out some way to deal with him. Things have improved at the hospital, but I'm not sure whether the changes in people are all for the better. I didn't mean to start gossiping. Idle talk starts all kinds of trouble. Do you want to see anything else?"

"A conversation like this isn't idle talk, Miranda. Sometimes it prevents trouble. You're a sensible woman. I've taken up enough of your time. "

Miranda smiled. "When you talk like that, you remind me of your father. You look more like your mother, but you talk like your father."

Stephen did not consider being told he talked like his father a compliment, but he could only assume that Miranda meant well. He wrote up the report as objectively as possible, listing the accomplishments that had taken place in the hospital in accordance with recommended procedure. He also decided to have another, hopefully friendly, fact-finding chat with Ralph Henry as to how he got his overseas news so quickly, and, in the meantime, try to find out why the professional Dr. Sampson, so obvious in his admiration of Dee Dee and reputedly aloof with the nurses, was making a point of driving Alice Hansen home.

CHAPTER FIVE

Stephen placed the carefully drawn and just completed map of the route to Northside Dam on top of the report on nurses' training, reflecting how inadequately black lines on white paper contrasted with the realities of experience. The overgrown path along the aqueduct had been surrounded by color, every imaginable shade of green, interspersed with red, orange, yellow and white flowers, which Alice had patiently identified. The penciled lines could not possibly describe the difficulties of following directions up, down and around Maroon Mountain as he led the way with his machete, the soil becoming damp and slippery as they neared the dam while overhanging branches full of thorns attacked them at every level. He found it much harder than he remembered to wield the machete. In his youth the machete seemed to be an extension of his arm, now it felt like a lead weight.

The map was nevertheless accurate, he felt, and should be easy to follow. Yet he longed for the artist's ability to depict the rapid scurrying of the ants, centipedes, millipedes and scorpions he disturbed while breaking trail and cutting back the bush. He looked up now at the copy of a medieval map that adorned the wall of his father's office, a distorted view of the New World, with sea monsters and leviathans awaiting their victims in the unknown Atlantic. Captain Warner would have dismissed depictions of the painful bites and stings of real attackers as unnecessary and infantile. Stephen reluctantly omitted them.

The machete Alice had provided proved invaluable, even in Stephen's inexpert hands. For long stretches the path was wide enough for careful footsteps, with plenty of underfoot evidence of the goats that enjoyed munching around the thorns of the acacia bush. Their invasive human footsteps and breathing had readily aroused the mosquitoes to buzzing and biting, especially when a tangled impasse required slashing and hacking in all directions in order to proceed. Despite ankle-length pants and long-sleeved shirts, they acquired multiple scratches and bites. Alice never uttered a word of complaint, so Stephen forced himself to hold his tongue. She actually seemed to enjoy the climb, pointing out wild orchids, a tamarind tree that had been there forever, and some soursop trees heavy with fruit. The few times the path was wide enough to walk side by side, Stephen found himself more distracted by her than the most brilliant foliage. The sun had penetrated the thick canopy of mahogany and tibbet trees with enough strength to redden Alice's face and make his cheeks burn. The physical discomfort did not diminish the exhilaration he felt when they finally sighted the greenish water of Northside Dam.

"What a strange green color the water is," Stephen said. "People are supposed to drink that?"

"It's just the reflection of the branches, the leaves are so thick. Don't you remember?" Alice knelt down on some flat stones and rinsed her face with the cool water by cupping her hands. "It's nice, clean water. We swam here all the time when we were kids."

Stephen surprised himself by saying, "Let's take a swim now."

Alice laughed. "Not today thanks. I want to get back on time. Mamy wasn't at all happy about my going off hiking this morning. Since it was you, and it was part of your job, she said all right. Let's just rest a few minutes, then start back. It should be easier going downhill."

To Stephen's relief they readily found a narrow downhill path, obviously created by the same goats that had munched back the acacia on the uphill trail. It stopped where the goats stopped, within sight of the well-packed dirt of Mahogany Road but a few yards short of it, so there was another stretch of hacking the thorny bush.

"We're blazing a trail for Americans to follow," Alice said. Stephen could think of no pertinent reply at the time, but had continued to ponder this remark as he produced several maps from his rough notes and drawings. Only after he pushed the squeaking old chair away from the desk and leaned back, was he able, from this precarious but comfortable position, to relax enough to compose an impersonal letter of resignation to be given to Captain Warner.

He reread it several times before placing it carefully below the maps and the Nurses' Training Report. He was not entirely satisfied, there was so much he couldn't say, but the wording was the best he could come up with. The letter conveyed politely yet firmly, with regret and appreciation, his intention to leave government service and return to the private practice of law. He could find no tactful way of protesting that he was not a mapmaker and did not wish to be a trailblazer, so he left these sentiments unexpressed. He certainly would not confess his growing concern that frustration was diminishing his self-respect and threatening his self-control. After all, he had suggested jumping into a mysterious green pond in the middle of an isolated forest never once thinking of the consequences, hoping that Alice Hansen might follow him. This was not the kind of abandon he condoned, wanted to remember, or risk repeating.

"Oh, there you are," Mark said, a matter-of-fact greeting that shattered his thinking. "Father's been looking all over for you. Wants to consult you on a legal matter. Wouldn't tell me what it was, but he looks concerned. Come see me when he's finished, I have some really good news."

"I'd welcome a tough legal problem, the tougher the better. I'm tired of these schoolboy exercises, doing nothing but drawing maps and writing reports. Getting cussed out by old ladies. Taking orders from someone who knows nothing about the concepts of law. Only rules and regulations."

"If the Administrator knew the law he wouldn't need you."

Stephen's only response was an angry look. He shuffled the papers on the desk in front of him into a neat pile, edges carefully lined up. Mark broke the silence. "So you finally located Northside Dam? I told you it wouldn't be difficult."

"It wasn't easy. It's all overgrown. I never would have found it without Alice's help."

"I've heard you're being seen with her all over the island."

"She was kind enough, despite her mother's objections, to spend her one day off helping me find the dam. After you refused. Tell your gossipers she's a childhood friend. I think Dr. Sampson's seen more of her than I have,"

"Really? That's odd. I've always seen him with Dee Dee. Here's Father. I'm off to see if the mail's come in."

"Good morning, Stephen. Are those our accounts you're working on?" Cedric Markham's usual air of distraction was accompanied by a worried frown.

"No. We agreed that Mark would do those, remember? It's only another hospital report for the Administrator, and a map of the old Northside Dam that he wanted."

"Oh, yes, yes. Wonderful project. Too bad the Danes never really completed it. I didn't know you could draw maps."

"I didn't know it either. It appears I have hidden talents."

"Well, don't be bitter about it. We should be grateful for any talent God give us to help serve our fellow man. You'll be seeing Captain Warner tomorrow?"

"Tomorrow morning."

"Good. There's something important I want you to discuss with him. Personally."

Stephen responded that his father saw the Administrator frequently at official functions but Cedric Markham insisted that his son, a lawyer, deal with this "private matter".

"This is not a business problem, but a legal one. I'm counting on you to make the Administrator see it that way. As you know, Bishop Hudson has been here from Antigua. That's why I've been so busy. Both the Bishop and our own Father Morrow believe that our local Anglican church should remain under the British Diocese of Antigua. You know the attitude of the American church toward the color question and the trouble it's caused in Puerto Rico. We've all agreed that, here in the West Indies, segregation in the churches should never be introduced," Cedric Markham said firmly.

"Captain Warner has given me the impression that he expected the Americans to take over in every sense," Stephen replied. "Look at the precedent you would be setting. If the Anglicans remain part of the English Church rather than become Episcopalians in the American Church, the Lutherans could remain part of the Danish Church."

"Stephen, I don't want you to argue *against* me, young man, but *for* me. Here in the Caribbean we're all mission churches, let us remain that way. We've been preaching the brotherhood of man for two hundred years. We Americans and Europeans joined the churches that were set up for local people, and now we presume to discriminate against the locals in their own churches? What kind of precedent are we talking about? Surely you can make Captain Warner see that maintaining the status quo is the best way to avoid trouble?"

Stephen agreed to do everything he could, suspecting that his father might have foreseen such jurisdictional problems in the church when he suggested that his son work for the Administrator. He begrudgingly admired his father's strategy. Stephen hoped that successfully arguing his father's request might facilitate his own resignation.

Mark came in announcing rough seas had delayed the arrival of the mail boat from Puerto Rico. He broke through the unresponsive silence abruptly. "Well, what do you think of the contract?"

"What contract?"

"Father, didn't you tell him? I thought it would be all settled and signed by the time I got back. Markham and Sons has been offered the dealership for Ford automobiles and there should be some coming in on the next Navy ship. Captain Warner approved bringing them in that way, because he believes more automobiles be a boon to the island in case of emergency now that war has been declared. The Navy's even arranging to pave some roads and allow us to buy gasoline from their storage tanks. As a part of the contract, we, as dealers, are going to get one of the cars at cost. The first civilian automobile. Imagine that!"

Cedric Markham said that he was about to discuss the contract, but had something more important to attend to first, a church matter. "Just check this contract over, will you, Stephen? Mark's been over it so many times I'm sure it's satisfactory. If you say it's all right, I'll sign it when I get back from the vestry meeting."

His father's obvious priorities were very much on Stephen's mind when he met with the Administrator on the following morning. Captain Warner seemed delighted to have information in the form of a map and responded graciously to Stephen's query regarding how things were going. "So it's been a quiet, uneventful week for you. Well, I must admit we're pretty far from the real action and I know these little reports can be tedious, but they must be done. It's a big advantage here that the people speak English. For a while, after we found out we were coming here, my wife was afraid the local people might speak Danish; she had had such a bad time in Panama with Spanish-speaking domestics. Finally, we were able to get some house-servants from the Caribbean, wives of canal laborers from Barbados or Jamaica. One of those islands. Millicent likes things to be done right and spends a lot of time training our servants. She certainly didn't want to waste her time learning Spanish."

"English has always been the *lingua franca* of the Caribbean," replied Stephen, "The language of trade, you know. Only a select few learned Danish, to help with administration. My mother, of course, speaks Danish well."

"But your father came from America?"

"My grandfather came from America when my father was young boy. My grandfather was a widower. He later married one of the daughters of the MacFarland family but they didn't have any children. My mother came here to visit her school friend, Lillian, who later married Fritz Loring."

"Enough, enough. I've heard how all the families are related. We have a lot of that in Virginia. Particularly in my wife's family, which goes back to Revolutionary days. Even though you have a Danish mother, I see no reason to doubt your loyalty to America, or should I?"

"Of course not, sir."

"We've all been officially warned about a big spy ring in Washington working from the German Embassy. Your father was born in Connecticut, wasn't he?"

"Yes, he was. On another subject, he requested I personally give you this message, sir."

Captain Warner's expression changed from affability to discomfiture as he read the letter. He stood up from his desk and walked over to the window overlooking the Christiansted harbor. The letter, grasped firmly in his hand, fluttered in the morning breeze, highlighted against the thick dark walls of his office. "Well, young man, you're the lawyer. What's the legal position on this?"

"There is no written law, sir, just custom. Tradition. With the exception of the Lutherans, the Danish state church, all the other churches were originally established here as missions to the African slaves. Two hundred years of tradition is a strong precedent. Indeed, formalization of tradition is the basis of law."

"Please speak plain English. Are you telling me that the churches here were established in the beginning for the colored and then they let the white people in?"

"That's pretty much the way it happened. These are small and for the most part, poor islands. Even at the height of the sugar trade when the planters got rich, the working people were poor. But the missionaries trained many freemen and slaves as builders and masons, so they built the chapels and churches by themselves, with their own hands, for their own use. You will recall, sir, that by the terms of the Transfer Treaty, the congregation belonging to the Lutheran Church--the Danish National Church--retains control of their church buildings, and their church funds, including the land they own in Christiansted and Frederiksted and throughout the island. So there's no legal precedence for interference. The Moravians, who established the first missions, own extensive properties. I checked the deeds. Extensive properties, along with simple structures."

"So you checked on the deeds and the Transfer Treaty too. Well, that's what I'd hope for and expect from a lawyer. Don't suppose the land's worth much or ever will be, but no one stinted on this Government House. It's one of the finest buildings I have ever worked in, and that includes Washington."

"This was built by Governor Von Scholten, in the days when the plantation owners and merchants were rich on sugar. We haven't been rich for almost a hundred years."

"So I hear everyday. Well, Stephen, at this time I am not predisposed to interfere in any way. I do believe in keeping the races separate, but I'm not much concerned with the practices of churches. Since you assure me the local custom has legal merit, I say, let the churches continue to do what they have been doing.."

"Thank you, sir. My father will be pleased."

"He may not be so pleased when he hears my other news. I don't want to stir up this church business because I have another potential problem. It will be public knowledge in a few days so you might as well tell your father now. Washington has concurred with my suggestion that there be no further meetings of the Colonial Council until the war is over."

"You mean there will be no self-government whatsoever?"

"If you care to phrase it that way. All authority must be centralized in the hands of the Navy to insure maximum security. I know your father is a member of the Colonial Council, so I hope he will use his influence to convince the council members of the wisdom behind this decision."

Stephen agreed to pass on the message.

"You don't look very happy about this," the Administrator said.

"We've always been rather proud of our Colonial Council. The status of serving on it and all that the council itself implies. Surely these islands need not be so worried about security that we have to employ such extreme measures."

"I must take every precaution. There *are* submarines out there, I am certain, maybe closer than we think, we won't know for sure until it's too late. I intend to be prepared for every eventuality. There is danger from within as well. People like Ralph Henry and his ilk. Congress doesn't realize what it's like in these outposts of America. The people here are different. Not like real Americans."

"An elective legislature was part of the intent of the Transfer Treaty. The rule of the people is the basic tenet of democracy."

"So the politicians say, but hardly practicable during a time of war. Especially amongst people who have no long standing tradition of democracy. I can only assume that you didn't know Ralph Henry's been in contact with the American Civil Liberties Union. A seditious group that does nothing but stir up a lot of trouble in Washington by taking advantage of the American legal system. Once these radicals get together----look at New York. Boston is worse, with that crazy Roger Baldwin. I understand that your childhood friend is in contact with the ACLU as well."

"My childhood friend?" Stephen tried not to sound bewildered.

"That's how Lieutenant Sampson described her to me yesterday. The Hansen woman. One of the nurse trainees. Her brother is a member of the Urban League and they correspond quite regularly."

"I wouldn't know. I've never discussed politics with Alice Hansen."

"Well, she certainly discussed them in detail with Lieutenant Sampson. Told him all about her brother, what he was doing and how Virgin Islanders in New York felt. I guess you don't ask the right questions. See if you can do better and keep Ralph Henry quiet, at least."

While handing over his report on the hospital, Stephen reminded the Administrator that Ralph Henry had agreed to cooperate on health issues, nothing more. At the same time Stephen deftly and surreptitiously removed his letter of resignation from among the papers. "You will notice that fever cases are way down, especially among infants," he said, slipping the letter into his pocket smoothly. "Here are some detailed sectional maps of the dam site."

"Good. My wife isn't feeling well today, so perhaps you can join us for lunch next week. I'm relying on you to keep things going smoothly."

On the ride back to Frederiksted Stephen decided that there were dimensions and ramifications of his job that he should have recognized earlier. He had been so absorbed in eradicating mosquitoes or locating a dam he had been blind to other issues, administrative and legal, involving the war. Alice Hansen and Lieutenant Sampson were obviously more attuned to national issues affecting the Virgin Islands than Stephen was, even with his title and position of Administrator's Assistant. While feeling over- qualified for an inconsequential job, he had grossly minimized its importance, been negligent in observation and imperceptive to the ramifications and possible consequences.

Humbled, he went in search of his father. Cedric Markham accepted the news of the dissolution of the Colonial Council with equanimity. He was more interested in the Administrator's decision to accede to the church's request. "You must have presented our case well. You're becoming a real diplomat. As for the Colonial Council, well, it's really a misnomer, isn't it? We're not a colony any more."

"My professional opinion would be that in a legal sense; we still are a colony," Stephen said.

"Well, remember what happened to the Romans in Judea. Colonial governments are transitory. The Church is permanent."

"As I recall, Roman governors caused quite a bit of trouble in Judea."

"The hell with Judea," Mark said. "That was almost two thousand years ago. I thought when the Americans came we would have proper elections and citizenship rights. Father, can't you do something about this?"

Cedric Markham said that protest would be futile while the islands remained in a state of emergency. Mark then appealed to Stephen, who answered, "The United States probably has more pressing concerns at the moment, like protecting the world for democracy".

"What about our democracy? They're taking it away!"

"Maybe you should get together with Ralph Henry," Stephen said. He felt powerless to bring about family reconciliation or argue with his usually placid brother.

"I'm not interested in local demagogues," Mark said. "I'm talking about educated and civilized people who should make the decisions for the common people. The way they do in Virginia."

Stephen and Cedric Markham looked at each other. Mark apparently noticed the quick exchange of glances. "I've been discussing these matters with Dr. Sampson. States have power in America. In Virginia, they have very effective state laws that keep Negroes from voting so that control remains in the hands of the landowners."

"Well, you could always get involved in local politics," Stephen said. "Like Father…"

"It would mean time away from the business," Mark said.

"You might have to give up your recreational time. Polo and such."

"I'm not joking, Stephen. It's important that people like us, the right families, the ones who know how things should be done, keep control of what goes on here. I'm sure that's why Father wanted you to work for the Administrator, so you could be an example of the well-trained, educated leader, while gaining practical experience in how America governs. I was the one who had to stay home, help with the business, while you went away to college and to study law. I was sacrificed so you could be a leader."

Stephen could only stare at his usually taciturn older brother. Cedric Markham said, "You told me you didn't want to go away, that you had all the academic preparation you ever wanted from that school in Antigua."

"That's true, I did say that. But I was too young to know what I was saying. You should have insisted. Now I feel inferior when I talk to people like Dr. Sampson and Karen. Stephen doesn't really care anymore about being with the people who used to be his friends or what happens to us. He changed in America."

Mr. Markham did not appear to be listening. "You have compared me to Abraham who was willing to sacrifice his son Isaac."

Mark protested that he never once thought about Abraham and Isaac and that sacrifice was the wrong word. "I want to be here. I know that Stephen didn't really care to work for the Administrator. He only did it to please you. I want to please you as well. But I don't want our way of life to change, not in the wrong way."

Cedric Markham roused himself from his reverie and looked directly at Stephen. "I'll admit it. I always thought that the law was the best preparation for politics."

"I'm sorry, Father. I'm not sure how I feel concerning a lot of the issues. Mark's right. I've changed. Lack of conviction makes a poor politician. I'm willing to support Mark of course, as long as he wants to fight for what he feels is right. One of the first things I learned in law school was the necessity of identifying your principal adversary, and try to outwit him. If that fails and you can't beat him, join him. If at all possible. If you do get involved in local politics, who would be a future adversary ?" Stephen said.

Mark barely hesitated. "Ralph Henry. And I can hear Beulah Heyliger shouting already."

"Of course. Without a doubt. And Ralph Henry's way ahead of you. The Administrator told me that he already has connections with something called the Civil Liberties Union and another organization. The Urban League. I made notes of the names. As far as Captain Warner is concerned, these organizations are on a par with German spies."

"There's no need to be sarcastic. Ralph Henry is a disgrace. An ungrateful bastard. After Father helped him go to Denmark and everything. Ralph should be helping me, not trying to become a leader himself."

"He probably went to Denmark, New York and Washington so he could become a leader. And studied the law and…"

"Father! How can you be so complacent? Don't you expect loyalty from a man you have helped so much?" Mark said.

"I doubt if Ralph Henry considers his ambitions being disloyal to Father."

"I didn't ask you. I asked Father."

"If you're going to get angry at the very beginning of a discussion, don't go into politics," Cedric Markham said. "It wears you out and you don't think clearly. Stephen says that you should learn how to outwit an adversary. In business, I learned never to make an enemy in the first place. Even you two heathens should know how Christians should feel about their enemies. Now I'm late for an appointment with the Bishop.

Here, Mark, take this. I've signed the contract for the automobile agency. Please put it in the mail. Maybe we'll actually get some cars shipped in here before they decide to eliminate commercial shipping altogether. Remember, the devil is our worst adversary and Jesus is our true advocate." Cedric Markham left quickly. His sons stared at his retreating back.

"He does that all the time, starts talking bible talk, and cuts off discussion," Mark said. He was no longer talking loudly, the strength and conviction had left his voice, and he flopped down limply in the chair opposite Stephen. "I'm ashamed to say that once he said he'd signed the contract for the car agency, I don't feel angry or indignant any more. Is it possible that all I really wanted was a car?"

Stephen laughed. "Life is not that simple. You probably want to impress Karen with a car. Or an interest in politics."

"All of you, Mother too, seem to be so aloof from what's going on here. None of you understand how I feel about this place. Just because I play tennis, polo, and go sailing doesn't mean I don't care about other people and what happens to them. Business has never been better. It's because the Americans are here. And they're at war. *We're* at war. Our tiny, little West Indian islands that have never invaded or bothered anyone. The life we've known is changing and I don't like the changes. Ralph Henry used to be our friend. He respected us. Didn't Father lend him money? Couldn't we foreclose on the newspaper or something?"

"No."

"What do you mean, no?"

"The worst thing you could possibly do would be to antagonize Ralph Henry. He's still fond of us. Fond of father, at least. American history shows us that successful politicians learn to make alliances everywhere."

"Oh, history," Mark said. "What does that mean to us, American history?"

"American power is shaping our destiny."

"How pompous you sound! Like a sermon by Father Morrow. Always talking about history '...redressing the balance in favor of the colored man.' Don't you care about your family, your friends, your home?"

"More than you'll ever know. I gave up a woman I truly loved because I loved my island more. Because I felt so tied to everyone and everything here."

"You mean that brief engagement you wrote home about? Mother said she didn't think it would work out. Father said it was time you were thinking about getting married. He says the same thing about me. But until now there was no one here I was interested in."

"It wasn't a brief engagement, and it was very serious. We were engaged for two years and I loved Dorothy very much. I couldn't imagine life without her. She was beautiful, intelligent, fun to be with. Everything I wanted, everything anyone could want. She graduated from Radcliffe and planned to be an art historian. I was so happy, so infatuated with her, I was wearing blinders."

"There was something wrong with her?"

"No... Not really wrong; different. It simply failed to occur to me that she wouldn't want to live in Saint Croix and it never entered her head that I had no intention of permanently residing in Boston. When I told her my plans she laughed and said it would be ridiculous to ever consider living on some little uncivilized island populated by people whose ancestors came from Africa. People who knew nothing about art and culture. I knew then it was over. My forefathers had made the choice to come here. Dorothy was rejecting all of us, everything we represented. Even if some of the things she said were true, I knew this was the place where I belonged."

"I'm pretty sure Karen doesn't feel that way. I've just realized there's not much chance she can go back to Denmark until the war is over. Mother says I should get to know Karen better, meaning longer, before I even begin to think seriously about marriage. The war has given me the chance to do that.

I've got to have something more to do with my life than just work in Father's business. I need to do something important. Like you. I want to know what's going on in the world. Let's both have dinner at home tonight so we can talk a little more about this. Are you seriously suggesting that Ralph Henry and I should consider ourselves political allies? I need your advice and your access to Government House. What's that you're tearing up?"

"Nothing. Just a letter I've decided not to deliver. Why don't you get that contract in the mail? Captain Warner is worried about how dependable mail deliveries are going to be in the future. Right now most communiqués go via dip-lomatic pouch to Saint Thomas, but we may soon have to rely on coded cables for official business. I'll see you later at dinner."

Stephen threw the tiny bits of his carefully worded resig-nation letter in the old wicker wastebasket and headed out toward the hospital. Perhaps he could find Alice, ask some questions, get some answers. He had no clear idea of what he wanted to do next, just a vague sense of the direction in which to go and a hope that he would find Alice when he got there.

CHAPTER SIX

"Good morning, Stephen. Will you, by any good fortune, be seeing Ralph Henry today?" Miranda Muckle greeted him from the front steps of the Frederiksted Clinic.

"Good morning to you, Nurse Muckle. Were *you* looking for *me*?" Stephen said, unable to resist teasing the Head Nurse, always so formal and disapproving when she stood guard inside her hospital fortress. But standing outside, she appeared alone and vulnerable, her white uniform a shining target bathed in the early morning sunlight. Stephen smiled at her as he mounted the steps.

"Well, yes, as a matter of fact I was looking for you," Miranda said. "I just wanted to thank you for whatever you said to Ralph Henry about Elias. He's begun to behave like a proper orderly. It's been a miracle. A genuine miracle. You can't imagine what a difference it makes to have the hospital running smoothly again. Everything clean and neat, the windows shut properly and opened again at the right time. And Elias smiling and wishing you 'good-day'. A miracle. Thank you."

"I'm happy for you, Miranda. It's nice to know that at least something is working out right. I'll be sure to pass on your message. I'm on my way to see Ralph Henry now."

Deciding it would be indiscreet to ask Miranda what time Alice would be finishing work, Stephen walked away. He had missed seeing her the day before, so assumed her hours of work had changed. Also, he wanted to preserve the memory of Miranda's gratitude to fortify him against Ralph Henry's expected criticism.

"Excuse me if I don't get up from my desk but I just want to finish this editorial about the sport of kings," Ralph Henry said after a nod of greeting. "Why weren't *you* playing polo last Sunday, over there at Granard with the rest of the royal families? Getting bored with our island life? I had to watch from the road, but no matter. Polo won't be here much longer."

"I just came to thank you on behalf of Miss Miranda Muckle. She says there has been a real change in Elias's behavior, a change for the better, for everyone at the hospital. She's very grateful to you for speaking to him."

Ralph Henry frowned. "Believe it or not, I never said a word to him. I meant to. But I forgot about Elias. The news about discontinuing meetings of the Colonial Council just put it out of my mind. That's the real news, taking away our Colonial Council. Not this phantom war, which they're using as an excuse to disenfranchise us."

Stephen was disinclined to discuss politics on a beautiful morning that had started out so well. He was not surprised that the information he was supposed to deliver about the ban on the meetings of the Colonial Council considered "confidential" by the Administrator was not news to Ralph Henry.

"Well, something happened. To Elias, I mean."

"Maybe the Americans bribed him. It's an effective tool when the people are impoverished."

"As a newspaper editor, you should be careful about slander."

"As a newspaper editor, I look for good stories. And as a lawyer, I've had more experience with slander than you have."

"Much more."

Ralph Henry dropped his pencil and stood up. Stephen, for once the calmer one, was amused by the realization that their usual roles were switched. Ralph Henry began to pace around the cluttered office verbalizing thoughts that would undoubtedly end up as an editorial.

"You and your kind criticize me for bad faith, you who consider yourselves a superior people. Are we natives so uncivilized that we don't have a conscience? We have models you probably don't even know about or have never heard of. W.E. Du Bois. James Weldon Johnson. Paul Lawrence Dunbar. Langston Hughes. What in the world of the arts have any of the white rulers here produced? How dare the Administrator presume we aren't capable of self-government? Are we the real sinners on this island? Or is it you, the "royal" families? Or is it the American master race? Why is our one miniscule piece of democratic machinery, our Colonial Council, being taken from us? War is being used as an excuse. War isn't a reality here. Only an excuse."

"Perhaps. But this morning I merely wanted to congratulate you on behalf of the Head Nurse at the hospital on a certain reformed sinner --Elias. I'll come back when you aren't so busy. I thought that you, of all people, would be glad to see the *Colonial* Council be replaced someday. Not dissolved. Replaced."

"What do you mean?"

"Sometimes a name signifies a lot. The war won't last forever. Why perpetuate the word 'çolonial'. As I said, I'll come back some time when you aren't so busy." Stephen left quickly while Ralph Henry was still silent, staring at him.

Finishing his short report on improvements in the hospital, Stephen noted it was not yet eleven o'clock. As midday approached, Stephen grew bored with inactivity. His father and brother were at least doing *something* while he sat alone in the office of Markham and Sons. He decided to walk home for luncheon with his mother so he could at least resolve one nagging worry. She had not appeared at dinner the previous evening, perhaps resorting to her own technique of control, using illness, real or feigned, for ending or avoiding arguments, as effective in its way as the biblical quotations her husband used for the same purpose.

Yet any change in his mother's daily routine was cause for concern as was the possibility that the illness might be serious. When Stephen joined her for a simple luncheon at La Grange, he felt both relieved by her presence at the table and guilt-ridden from the warmth and affection of her welcome, the smile of a person too often and too long alone.

"Whatever possessed you to walk home in the noonday heat?" Kristin Markham said. "I am going to keep on insisting that your father buy a second carriage for you--and me--to use. He's the one who wants you to go back and forth to Christiansted and work for him as well. Besides, I don't mind spending most of my time at home, but I certainly dislike the idea that I can't get away if I want to. We need two carriages now. For my health and your convenience."

"Well, actually, I didn't spend the morning working for Father. I stopped by the hospital and then I went over to speak to Ralph Henry for a few minutes."

Kristin Markham conveyed her disapproval of the visit by calling Ralph Henry a man of menace with no kindness in him.

"I just stopped by to thank him on Miranda Muckle's behalf for the improvement in Elias's behavior. Then it appeared that Ralph wasn't responsible for the change after all."

"Of course not. I know what happened. For heaven's sake, why didn't you ask me? Elias's cousin Humphrey just got back from Panama. His mother died and left him some property and the notary located him in Panama. Humphrey is going around telling everyone who will listen that this new doctor here saved his life down there while he was working on the Canal. This new doctor, whatever his name is, was the only doctor who visited the laborers' wards himself. He saw to it that they received good care, clean sheets and proper doses of medicine. Didn't leave all that to the nurses."

"Humphrey told you all this?"

"No, of course not. Humphrey told Gustav. Gustav told me. You do remember Gustav? He's been our gardener since you and Mark were little boys. The doctor made sure that the families were provided for too, when the laborers were too ill with fever to work. Humphrey told Elias--- they're cousins-- and everybody else in the family about this doctor. That's what made the change in Elias. He thinks the Americans are good people now. At least, some of them are. And if I ever were to go to a doctor, it would be that one."

"Well, that's certainly a plausible explanation. Thanks for telling me."

"You think I don't know anything that's going on, just because I stay home most the time. The birds tell me. Oh, Stephen, don't look so somber. When you look that way, you're no fun at all. You deserve to be teased. You tease everyone else."

When Stephen protested that he was serious person with a serious job, his mother said she hoped his work was serious enough to compensate for his absence and repeated that they needed another means of transportation.

"You're tired, aren't you? Is it that walk in the sun? "

Stephen said he wasn't tired, just frustrated and confused. "These people! I really don't understand them. They complain when people are trying to help them. Everybody blaming everyone else. Tell me again how you heard all this about Dr. Hokansen."

"It was the gardener. I see more of him than I do of my own family, which isn't *my* fault. He knew the Navy doctors were friends of yours and Mark's. Gustav is family to Elias, and they're both family to Humphrey. Humphrey isn't family to Ralph Henry, though. That's how I knew and Ralph Henry didn't. Ralph Henry likes to think he knows everything, but he doesn't, even though he's got spies everywhere, even in the telegraph office. This time I knew something he didn't."

"I guess I'd learn more if I just stayed home," Stephen said. "You don't happen to know if Ralph Henry has a spy in Government House and who he is?"

"No, I don't know that. Is Dr. Hokansen the one who goes to Granard with Mark?"

"No, that's the other one, the younger one, Lieutenant Sampson. Lieutenant Hokansen is older, the one with those remarkable paintings I told you about."

"Do you think he's really interested in art? He sounds like a nice man, a good man."

"Don't sound so doubtful. He *is* a nice man, and now that you've heard it from a reputable source like the gardener's cousin, you know he's a conscientious doctor. Why are you so suddenly interested in doctors, you who hate to talk about them?"

"Don't be sarcastic with your mother, Stephen. I need some kindness and consideration. And a little more attention."

"We're all very concerned about you, all of the time. You refuse to talk about your health and are determined to do everything your own way..."

Kristin then confessed that she had hurt herself gardening. A small stone had pierced the soft flesh just above her knee when she was kneeling and some dirt had gotten in it. Despite a thorough cleansing and the application of aloe, it pained her when she awoke the following morning and now she had difficulty walking.

"We're going to the hospital right away. You know about blood poisoning. We have horses, for God's sake. You know that soil around horses is contaminated with tetanus."

"I wasn't near the stables. I was in the garden."

"And what does your gardener Gustav fertilize the garden with? I'm going to town to get the carriage. I'll be right back. Then we're going to the hospital."

"No. I don't want to go now. I don't want you upsetting your father and Mark. I don't want people to see me going to the hospital. You know how they talk. They'll say I'm dying, and if people do around saying you're dying, you feel you have to oblige them. Perhaps a doctor could come here..."

Stephen tried to keep the alarm out of his voice. "The hospital. Now."

"No. I'll go first thing in the morning, early before anyone is up and about. Don't tell your father. Don't tell Mark. I will see that doctor, the one from Panama, and no one else. And tell Miranda Muckle to see to it that no one bothers me. If there's going to be a fuss, I just won't go and that's all there is to it. I can't bear people around me getting all excited. In fact, it makes me ill just to think about it. Either you and I go in quietly early tomorrow morning or I don't go at all."

Stephen, noting the resolute expression on his mother's face, acquiesced. He spent the rest of the day and most of a restless night worrying about the infection spreading through his mother's body, and, at the same time, getting more and more annoyed by the secrecy imposed upon him. Fortunately, both Cedric and Mark Markham spent the night in the town house but sent the carriage back home for Stephen's use, so the need for subterfuge was minimalized.

By morning his mother had such difficulty walking that she allowed Stephen to carry her down the stairs and out of the house.

"You're right. We should get another carriage, a more comfortable one," Stephen said. "Mark is talking about getting a car."

"That would be wonderful for you, but I don't want to lose our horses. I love horses. Thank goodness, you've hitched up Esmeralda, she's a gentle horse and knows how to avoid the bumps in the road. I used to ride her, when we were both younger. Sometimes I wished she would run away with me, up to the hills, but she never did."

"Why did you wish that?" Stephen said, noting that his mother's face was flushed and her eyes glittering. He longed to put his hand on her forehead but refrained, afraid that she might classify any protective gesture on his part as "fuss" and change her mind about going to the hospital.

"Oh, I don't know. I was young and bored I guess, homesick maybe, desperate in a way. Esmeralda had more sense than I did. She wouldn't run then, and I couldn't run now, even if I wanted to."

"You'll be able to walk and run again. Don't worry."

"I didn't mean that. It's just that I'm tied to the land now, more like a plant than an animal."

"You're neither. You're a free human being, capable of making your own decisions."

"So your father says. That's why I refuse to go to the English church. That's why I got tired of going. Tired of listening to your father, standing up there, reading some lesson from Isaiah-- how he loves to quote Isaiah-- saying that patience is a virtue, then Father Morrow droning on and on about the true freedom man finds by following the teachings of Jesus. Neither your father nor Jesus ever gave me freedom. I never felt free. I was more like Esmeralda. A gentle horse. I did the things I was trained to do, was expected to do. But I did escape. I refused to become an animal. I became a plant instead."

When Stephen, inarticulate due to his increasing anxiety, did not respond Kristin Markham lapsed into silence. As they approached town, the streets were filling with people who would recognize the Markham carriage and strive for a glimpse of its occupants. Kristin had closed her eyes and did not seem to be aware of them.

Fortunately, she did not know about the curious patients watching for submarines. Their view of the sea included a sweeping survey of Strand Street, so the vigilant would spot her arrival immediately. Stephen also worried about the effect her wild musings might have on Lieutenant Hokansen, a man who had admitted his main interest was the collection of scientific data and described himself as pragmatic.

The attempt to go directly to the doctor's office was foiled by Miranda Muckle who was standing just inside the front door. "Why, Miss Kristin, how nice to see you! Your foot is sick, I see."

"It's not her foot, it's her knee. Maybe the whole leg," Stephen said.

"You're forgetting your Cruzan, Stephen. For us 'foot' means leg. Well, foot, knee or leg, the doctor will fix that up for you right away, Miss Kristin. Carry her right into his office, Stephen. Careful you don't knock her foot against the side of the doorway. I'll fetch Dr. Hokansen. Here, sit in this comfortable chair."

Kristin Markham immediately gave her attention to the pictures on the wall and her gaze did not swerve as Miranda and Stephen eased her into the chair. She seemed so entranced Stephen wondered if seeing the paintings had been her real motive for insisting on seeing Dr. Hokansen rather than requesting her old friend Dr. Ramlov.

Dispatched to wait in the hallway while the doctor examined the wound, Stephen was soon joined by his father.

"What is going on? What has happened to your mother? Elias said you had to carry her into the hospital."

"Good morning, Father. Please don't shout. Mother's leg was hurting and this morning she wanted to see a doctor. It was painful for her to walk, so I carried her."

"See a doctor! She never wants to see a doctor. You know that. It must be serious. Why do I have to be informed that my wife is seriously ill by a hospital custodian?"

"We've only been here a few minutes and I didn't get a chance to tell you...oh, I see Elias found Mark as well. The whole town must know by now. Just what Mother didn't want."

Dr. Hokansen came out into the hall before Mark joined in the demand for explanations. "This is your father, Stephen? Nice to meet you, Mr. Markham. And your brother Mark? I've heard Dr. Sampson speak of you."

"How is my wife?" Cedric Markham demanded impatiently.

"At the moment she is quite relaxed, enjoying my paintings. Alice Hansen is with her, a nurse she requested to see."

"What is wrong with her? Why can't she walk?"

"An infected knee. Has Mrs. Markham been taking any kind of medication?"

"Not to my knowledge," Cedric Markham said, glancing at Stephen suspiciously. "Perhaps my son knows more than I do."

Stephen shook his head.

"Well, I'm not making a diagnosis, just voicing a possibility. Your wife may be a diabetic, what you call here 'the sugar disease'. I've seen quite a few cases since coming to Saint Croix. It seems that people treat it with local remedies that disguise the symptoms, so it's often hard to detect. But if that should be the case, if Mrs. Markham is diabetic, this small wound can be quite serious. The healing will be slow, there will be a tendency to ulceration, and the possibility of gangrene..."

"Gangrene! You mean blood poisoning. You can't be serious." Cedric Markham said.

"I don't want to alarm you. Nurse Muckle is trying to convince Mrs. Markham to give us a urine sample, but if what I suspect is true, that she's been keeping her sugar disease under control in some way, it won't be a reliable test. She is careful, I assume, in her diet. Not many sweets. That sort of thing."

"It's that bush tea," Mark said. "It's that bush tea. I know it is. Alice Hansen used to bring it to her and then Gustav learned how to grow it. All the old people around here make a tea of the leaves for too much sugar in the blood."

"Do you think you can get me a sample of the leaves? Thank you. Mr. Markham, when did you first notice anything that might make you think your wife was ill?"

After some hesitation, Cedric Markham admitted that he first noted the onset of illness in his wife about twenty years ago. "At least, about twenty years ago she began to change. It never occurred to me that she was ill and I'm still not sure that was the case. I just thought she was beginning to settle down--and about time, too--she had two children to take care of. She lost interest in partying, stopped wanting to go everywhere and do everything the way she did when she was younger. She did begin to tire easily, wanted to stay home from church and tried to avoid being upset in any way."

"That long! In all those years she never saw a doctor?" Dr. Hokansen made no effort to hide his surprise.

"She saw one. She was extremely thin, thinner than she is now. Dr. Ramlov prescribed a meat diet, which made her feel sicker. Finally, they compromised on oatmeal and cabbage soup as the basis of her diet."

"She saw only one doctor?"

"At that time Dr. Ramlov was the only doctor here. He's a Dane and she trusted him as much as she trusted any doctor after her friend Lillian Loring died. *He* didn't disapprove of the bush tea. *She* said it made her feel better. She said she was all right as long as she could live quietly. I did what she wanted. I stopped talking to her about my business problems. I was distressed about her lack of faith, but I tried my best to do as she wanted. Now it appears that I have doing the wrong thing. My God, doctor, when I married Kristin she was healthy, full of life. At first, I thought the children were too much for her. We got a nursemaid. The children went away to school as soon as they were old enough, but she never..."

"Mr. Markham, this is in no way your fault. On the contrary, both you and Mrs. Markham probably did the right thing. We have no cure for the sugar disease yet, nor any scientifically approved remedy either. Somehow, the people here discovered an herb that kept the disease under control. The danger was in deciding on the right amount, the right strength to use, how long to brew the tea. Too much could be dangerous, too little ineffective."

"It was our neighbor, Mr. Hansen who first recommended it. He's a chemist. Trained at the rum factory, " Mark Markham said.

Dr. Hokansen nodded. "You were right to remove as much worry as possible. If Mrs. Markham has been leading a normal life, even though it's a quiet one, it's best to continue with whatever she's been doing until we know better. Our concern for the moment is healing the wound. She should have expert nursing care and she doesn't want to stay in the hospital."

"She must have a nurse at home," Cedric Markham said. "The best one you have."

"It isn't that simple. Our trainees are needed here. In any case, I must ask you all to leave now. I can only repeat that Mrs. Markham's cure begins with keeping her calm and relaxed. Stephen, if you could come back in an hour?"

Cedric Markham strode off without a work of farewell. Mark lingered with Stephen on the front steps of the clinic. "I knew he'd blame me for bringing her here," Stephen said.

"Then Dr. Hokansen makes it worse by asking me, not Father, to come back. But I had to do it the way mother wanted, or she wouldn't have come to the hospital at all."

"You know Father," Mark said. "And don't blame the doctor for asking for you. I'm sure that's what Mother told him to say. Don't tell me you haven't noticed how you're the one she wants to do everything. She knows you'll do as she says. Don't worry about Father. He doesn't like to say anything when he's angry, that's why he rushed off that way. Gone back to the office to calm down, say a few prayers."

"He looked very angry. I'm sorry about that."

"I think he was shocked as well as angry. I'm sure it never occurred to him that Mother was physically ill. I never thought so. Did you?"

Stephen said that he had always worried about his mother and felt that his father neglected her and spent more time in church than with his wife. "When I came home from America she had become a recluse. She once told me that you can't transplant flowers from one climate to another without unexpected changes taking place, and I felt she was talking about herself. I remembered all this talk about transplants when Dorothy told me she felt she could never survive in the tropics."

"That's all nonsense, just an excuse. We're all immigrants, transplants, and most of us prosper. Your Dorothy just didn't love you enough. I don't want to hurt your feelings, but I sometimes think you're turning into a recluse yourself."

"Me? A recluse? That's nonsense. I'm out all the time, dealing with all kinds of local people. That's part of my job."

"A social recluse. You're ignoring your family and friends. Your old friends ask about you all the time. Lily Loring especially. You and she were pretty close before you left, and you've barely spoken to her since you've been back."

"I didn't mean to offend Lily. I've always liked her, the way she laughed at everything, had a lot of spirit. She was just determined to have a lot of fun. And wanted other people to have fun too. Maybe you're right. I was pretty depressed about losing Dorothy, and then Father got me this time-consuming job, and then Mother..."

Mark said that he was relieved to find that his mother's illness was physical. "I've been afraid she had some sort of mental illness that could be inherited, made me hesitate to think about getting married. Although now that I think about it, maybe the 'sugar disease' is inherited too."

"I doubt it. In your case, anyway. You're the healthiest person I know. Are you thinking seriously of getting married? The Danish girl? "

Mark admitted that he was thinking about although he was not sure how Karen felt. "She's awfully pretty, don't you think? And I should think Mother would like having another Dane in the family. But there's always money. Setting up another household, all of that. It's been easy, living at home. I don't think the business could support all of us, living separately, not the way we live now. Despite all we talked about last night, I guess I'll just have to forget about politics."

"Might as well, until the war is over. But you and Father have been predicting a boom in business due to the Navy and all they're doing here..."

"Yes, it does look like business is getting better. For us, at least. As for the planters...boom and bust. Boom and bust. That's the way it always has been with sugar and rum. That's why our frugal old grandfather went into importing and selling in the first place. For all their high living, I suspect we have more capital than the Macfarlands with all their property. By the way, did you see what Ralph Henry wrote about our innocent little polo game?"

"Not yet."

"Something about polo being the sport of kings and that we, the four families, behaved like royalty. How do you like that?"

Stephen laughed. "I think it's funny. Ten years of drought, one bad hurricane. Near bankruptcy half the time. Not my idea of the royal life."

"I'm off to the office to check on our finances. Let me know about Mother."

When Dr. Hokansen located Stephen waiting on the front steps, he invited him into his office. Kristin Markham looked relaxed, even contented.

"I've never seen such beautiful paintings," Kristin said. "They express what I've always felt about the harmony of man and nature. Nature is so close to us here in the tropics. Plants don't die in winter. Shed a few leaves perhaps, but with care they live on and on."

"That's just what I've been telling you, Mrs. Markham," Dr. Hokansen said. "Good care makes all the difference. We've been having quite a go-around here with your mother, Stephen. She absolutely refuses to stay in the hospital. I even offered to hang one of the paintings in her room. If she goes home, she must have a nurse. That ulcerated leg must be watched closely and the bandages changed frequently. A job for a trained nurse, and we have none to spare."

"Perhaps one of the trainees. Aren't they due to graduate soon?"

Dr. Hokansen explained that the trainees would just be graduating from one phase of their training and all of them wanted to continue. "Nurse Muckle picked good candidates. One even hopes to go to New York for some specialized training. Well," he said as he turned to Kristin Markham, "I'll have to let you go since you insist. But you must come in again tomorrow morning and by that time we will try to work something out. Let me get Nurse Muckle to help you out."

Dr. Hokansen paused for a moment before leaving the room. "I don't want to get your hopes up but significant research is being done in the treatment of the sugar disease. In Canada as well as in America. So we may come up with a cure, or at least an effective treatment soon. If you will just do exactly as you are told, Mrs.Markham, we may be able to help you soon."

Kristin nodded but Stephen saw the appeal in his mother's eyes, and quickly declined a wheelchair or other help. He carried his mother out to the carriage.

Kristin Markham discussed the paintings all the way home, seemingly oblivious to her bandaged leg. "Wouldn't it be wonderful to paint like that? How I wish I had had some training!"

"You told me you had drawing lessons as a young girl."

"Oh, I had drawing lessons and sewing lessons and singing lessons and never really learned anything. Just enough skills to make me a desirable wife. I guess I wasn't a very good one...not much of a mother either, I suspect. Never cared much about cooking and feeding people. I don't really like the smell of food."

Stephen was surprised by these rare confidences, which contrasted with his childhood memories of endless family dinners with all the aunts, uncles and cousins eating and eating.

"Mark and I love you just as you are. We wouldn't want you any other way."

"Dr. Hokansen tells me that these same flowers exist throughout the tropics. He's been to South America and seen hundreds of species. Made some sketches too, he said. Hybrids are the most beautiful, so delicate-looking, but he also says that some of them are very strong. If bred properly, they resist disease. I suspected that from the few Gustav and I were able to grow. They last longer, not just one day, like our native hibiscus." Stephen commented that she and Dr. Hokansen had spent more time talking about flowers than her illness, but Kristin Markham refused to be teased. "It's reassuring to have a scientific person say the same thing you've always believed. It's not very pleasant, you know, having people treat you as if you're half-crazy."

"Mother! No one has ever treated you that way."

"Well, they haven't taken me seriously. I promised that nice young doctor I'd take him one of my hybrid hibiscus tomorrow. I have one just like the one I saw in the painting. The yellow one with the pink center and the red stripes. It's just about ready to bloom. Tomorrow it should be ready. If it is, I'll take it to him. But you have to go with me. I don't want your father fussing over me, making a big spectacle."

If bringing in a few hibiscus was the excuse his mother needed for going willingly to the hospital, Stephen was ready to accept it. His anxiety about his mother's health was being replaced by resentment, caught as he was between his mother's repugnance for fuss and his father's obvious displeasure about being excluded from taking care of her. Cedric Markham solved of Stephen's problem at dinner.

"You don't have to worry about taking your mother to the hospital tomorrow, Stephen. I've arranged for Dr. Hokansen to come by here. And Alice Hansen will be coming in every day, to take care of your mother for as long as she is needed. I haven't informed your mother yet, she was sleeping when I came in and I didn't want to disturb her. "

"Mother likes Alice Hansen and hates to go to the hospital," Mark said.

Stephen agreed, wondering how his father accomplished what the doctor had deemed impossible.

"The Administrator also said he would appreciate it if you would come to Christiansted the first thing tomorrow morning, before you go anywhere else," Cedric Markham said, solving the mystery of how and through whom his requests had been granted. "He needs you to spend most of the day there. Something about an Act of Congress with new rules on import and export duties for both Puerto Rico and the Virgin Islands. I'm interested in the provisions of the legislation myself. It's important for anyone in business, not just our family. So I'm counting on you to do whatever the Administrator needs to have done. Are you listening to me, Stephen?"

"Sorry, sir. Yes, I was listening. I'll go first thing in the morning. May I use our carriage?" Stephen tried to cover up his momentary lapse of attention. He was wondering what it would be like to have Alice Hansen in his parents' home, seeing her every day.

"Yes, if you'll drop Mark off at the office. I'll stay here until the doctor and the nurse arrive, then go back into town with Dr. Hokansen. I want to talk with him privately. You just carry on your work with the Administrator in Christiansted. I'll take care of your mother."

CHAPTER SEVEN

Stephen arrived at the appointed hour and found Captain Warner waiting, obviously agitated and frowning with displeasure, his thick eyebrows bristling above angry gray eyes. "I appreciate your punctuality," he said. "These people. These people. No sense of the value of time. Well, here's a copy of the Jones Act--that's what it's called, these politicians love to name things after themselves--a new Act of Congress with different rules on import and export duties. I think the merchants and planters, including your father, will find them to be fair. Not so many changes, really. More of a clarification, I'm told. Certainly uses a lot more paper. Look it over and tell me what you think. And then summarize it in one short paragraph of simple English."

Stephen glanced at some of the pages listing figures and percentages. It was going to be necessary to compare them with earlier listings and until that tedious and dull job was finished, no informed opinion could be offered.

"I have given you a second copy," the Administrator continued. "For Ralph Henry. Just give it to him for his newspaper. He obviously has a friend in the cable office. There have been leaks from cables addressed to me that somehow become general knowledge and we're going to have to change over to coded messages. Something I should have implemented in the first place. There's a war on, though you'd never know it from the way these people are behaving."

Stephen now understood the reason for the Administrator's bad humor and in what he hoped was conciliatory tone remarked that coded messages were definitely a good way to deal with local spying.

"Spying? It's not spying. These people don't know how to go about spying. No, it's that Ralph Henry getting his friends and relatives to find out what's going on so that troublemaker can print it in his newspaper. After all, the people here have had plenty of practice snooping around. There is no gratitude for all we're doing for them. Now we're going to be risking American lives to protect them. Ingrates, all of them"

Stephen felt no desire to calm the Administrator. "According to Ralph Henry, a local group has petitioned to serve in the military, an offer to serve and protect their America. Protect *us*, not *them*."

"Yes, I know. Them, us. Us, them. Same damn problem as in Panama. You can't mix in all these colored people with the regular military. Perhaps we *could* train a local militia, but how do we instill a sense of discipline? Do they have one? Regardless, like the good public functionary that I am, I have sent their request on to Washington. Never thought I'd be sitting behind a desk in wartime."

Stephen did not trust himself to carry on an equable conversation with such a profoundly angry man. Hoping to be dismissed he asked what, if anything, he could do.

"After you've completed the summary of the Jones Act, research the latest rulings on the citizenship issue. Are these people bona fide American citizens? See if there's some ruling concerning non-citizens serving in the military in wartime. Ferret out what Ralph Henry's connections are in Washington. It's probably those radicals in the Civil Liberties Union. We might as well voluntarily give him the information he's getting anyway, so we can't be accused of doing things in secret."

"I agree," Stephen said.

"And another thing. Congress has given the Naval Administration an appropriation of one hundred thousand dollars to aid in carrying out our local administration. In other words, they've given it to me. In my legal capacity as Administrator, of course. Don't look so shocked. You're a trained lawyer, for God's sake. You are, after all, my legal adviser. What is it you do in your father's office anyway?"

Stephen acknowledged that the majority of his work was, for the most part , reviewing and revising contracts.

"I need you here in my office to do something far more important than that. With this new money I can offer you a full-time job with a decent salary," Captain Warner said.

Stephen listened with annoyance and surprise while the Administrator pointed out that both Stephen's father and brother could read contracts and their business had far less importance than foreseeing legal complications of directives he, as the Administrator, might have to generate. "They call this a military government, but it isn't really. We're just a few military officials charged with keeping order among civilians who have neither desire nor inclination to follow orders. I have no established precedents. Without precedents, I must consider consequences."

"You're creating precedents, sir. Making history."

"Is that what I'm doing? I'm glad you feel that way, because half the time I don't know myself. I thought I was being nothing more than a good American, a good Navy man, and then I find this hate sprouting up around me. It must be stopped. So what about it? Are you willing to take the position?"

Stephen requested some time to work things out with his family. With a heavy sigh, the Administrator rose from the desk and walked over to the window. His usually erect posture deserted him as he turned back to look at Stephen. The tone of command was gone from his voice as he said, "Of course. Glad you consider your family. My poor wife is worried sick about our son. Thank God he's been assigned to a desk job in Virginia for the time being. At least he won't be exposed to the risks of tropical diseases in some semi-civilized place where they even resist killing mosquitoes."

Captain Warner sat down at the desk before he continued "My wife. For years she did everything correctly, was the perfect hostess. Took the time to plan the nicest tea parties for the ladies, formal dinners and even tennis parties. You could forget that all around us they were digging up thousands of tons of mud and people were dying left and right of fever. That's what I consider carrying on. But now she is faced with the fact that our son's involved in the war and we're so far way. She doesn't seem to care about keeping up appearances. And that's part of our job." The indignation and tone of command disappeared as the Administrator added, in a plaintive after-thought. "You'll stay for luncheon, won't you? Is there chance I can convince you to relocate to Christiansted? It would be much more convenient to have you nearby."

"Not right away." Stephen was about to explain about his mother's illness, but remembered she didn't want the subject discussed. "My father has been thinking about buying an automobile. That would make things easier. Going back and forth, I mean."

"Good idea. I'd like to see more automotive transport on this island. Perhaps have a car for my personal use. With a car you could serve both towns. I need you to be mobile, to move around. That would be part of your new responsibilities. You'd like that, wouldn't you?"

"It interests me, of course, sir. But as I said, I'd prefer to discuss it with my family."

"Of course, of course. I'm encouraged to see you have this strong sense of family. But then, you're one of the royal families, aren't you?"

"I see you do read Ralph Henry's newspaper."

"Every word. I find it amusing. Most of the time. Amusing, yet equally and potentially dangerous. So keep your eye on him."

"I am doing my best, but I doubt that I have much influence. And I can't dispute the truth."

"Meaning?

"The United States Virgin Islands *are* under military rule."

"Certainly." Captain Warner was sitting erect again. "I'll never dispute that. It's nothing to be apologetic about. We purchased these islands to protect the Canal in time of war, and now we are at war, and we're hell bent on accomplishing what we're supposed to do. By God, I'm certainly going to apologize for doing my duty. I'm to see that the job is done right. The Virgin Islands are damn lucky to have the protection of the United States. Congress has given the President the power to '...direct policies, regulate insular officials and federal appropriations'. Review that legislation. Memorize it. Quote it during your get-togethers with the other royal families. Be sure that Ralph Henry's made aware of it. I suppose it's too much to hope he'll ever stick to the cold hard facts, but perhaps you can make *somebody* see that this kind of absolute control benefits these islands. Absolute means faster. It cuts out most of the red tape they're so fond of in Washington."

"What some people call 'red tape' others call 'checks and balances.'"

"You're supposed to argue for me, not against me. Let me know as soon as possible what your decision is. About the full-time position, I mean."

Stephen knew he would have no choice but to accept the Administrator's offer, though he did want to consider the consequences. He had always known his father expected to be repaid in some manner for providing his younger son with a lawyer's education. Cedric Markham had made it clear in manifold ways that money should only be spent with specific goals in mind. He had repeatedly hinted that his son should become influential through political involvement and had subsequently pressured him into working for the Naval Administration. Stephen suspected that in some medieval manner, his father hoped that any influence his son might acquire could be used to strengthen the role of the Anglican Church relative to island policy. His brother Mark, considering marriage, was now implying that he should have full responsibility and recompense for his faithful services to the family business. Stephen, as the lawyer in the family, could always provide pro-bono legal expertise but hardly merited a full-time job with the commensurate salary. Markham and Sons had always managed to successfully avoid contract disputes and labor problems. After all, the riots of 1878 had taken place in a different world and remote time. But, as Ralph Henry well knew, the memory of that violence could be invoked at a moment's notice to produce an atmosphere of tension in dealings between employers and workers. Cedric and Mark Markham obviously knew how to run a business successfully in Saint Croix. On the other hand, the Administrator had just admitted that he was concerned about his own success.

Stephen realized that his mother, who had been so demanding of his presence since his return, would no longer have to depend on him to the same degree. The daily presence of Alice Hansen as nurse and companion in the Markham plantation house changed the whole equation and gave Stephen a sensation of relief and freedom. He could foresee new glimmers of light in the pervading gloom of the household and cheerful conversation where there had been nothing but depressing silence and unwelcome mandates from his father.

As Stephen expected, Cedric Markham received the news of Captain Warner's offer with confident satisfaction and urged his son to take the position. "I've arranged for your mother to be well taken care of. Kristin has always been fond of the Hansen girl and I'm well acquainted with her parents, as you know."

"At some point I may find it necessary to move to Christiansted," Stephen said in an effort to focus the conversation on his own changing status. "Of course, that wouldn't be required if I have proper transportation."

"Good, good," Mark interrupted. "Maybe we could sell the Administrator some automobiles. Are we going to buy one for ourselves, Father? They did offer us a discounted price."

"I'm seriously considering it," Cedric Markham said. "Just let me check on the costs, factor in the shipping and see if we can afford one."

"Mother could use one to get out more," Stephen said.

"I'm well aware of that," his father said coldly. "Your mother has always been and will remain foremost in my thoughts."

"I think it's excellent news about your job, Stephen," Mark said. "Now that Mother's feeling a little better, I'm going to ask her to invite Karen for tea. The Navy placed four new orders with us this morning. We should be doing well financially for a year at least. And now that war is officially declared, the American Navy is bound to protect our shipping. We may even get rich."

"Don't say that out loud," Stephen said. "Ralph Henry would love to call us war profiteers."

"Nonsense, nonsense," Cedric Markham said. "I don't think Ralph Henry would ever call me a profiteer."

"Of course not, Father," Mark said. "Stephen was joking. Everyone knows how much you've helped Ralph Henry. The Administrator must be impressed with your work, Stephen. I hear that Mrs. Warner likes you. Any hints as to how I can please both of them? Karen would love to be invited to one of those Government House social functions."

Stephen said that the Administrator appreciated efficiency and punctuality and Mark said he would keep that in mind.

A week later a shipment of cars arrived and Mark was efficient in doing the paper work to accept delivery and prompt in bring one home to exhibit to the family as they were assembling for dinner. They came out into the courtyard to examine the automobile Mark displayed like a trophy.

"It's beautiful, isn't it? What do you think, Stephen? You've seen lots in Boston, I know. Do you like it, Father? Do you want to sit in it, Mother? I can help you get in."

"I'll wait," Kristin said. "But yes, I like the looks of it. Sturdy looking. Are all the cars alike?"

"The six in this first shipment are all alike, black with four doors. Four of them will go to the Navy. Maybe you'll get use of one, Stephen. This one is ours; isn't it, Father? The cousins are going to be so impressed. They may have a lot of horses but we have a motorcar. I hope I can use it on Sunday so I can drive Karen here for tea. You won't need it on Sunday, will you, Father? After church, I mean?"

"I don't even know how to drive the thing," Cedric Markham said. "How did you manage to learn so quickly?"

"Lieutenant Sampson showed me. Driving it is quite simple. He says the Navy has issued instructions to continue driving on the left hand side of the road to avoid accidents. The Danes have always done it that way and the donkey carts are used to it."

"God forbid that an American car should kill a Cruzan donkey," Stephen said.

"Driving a car's a lot easier than dealing with a temperamental horse or a stubborn donkey," Mark said. "Come on, Stephen, I'll show you."

Stephen was surprised by his brother's confidence as they drove slowly down the narrow dirt road into town. Mark did not grip the steering wheel but guided the car deftly and was relaxed enough to converse on a topic of importance. "The time has come for Mother to meet Karen. I know Mother doesn't want to meet new people, but this is the woman I hope to marry and it must be done. I want everything to go just right, so I need your help. After all, Karen is familiar with Danish court life and I don't want us to look like ignorant colonials. Father will want me to drive us all to church Sunday morning, you know that. He may be frugal and all that, but it's nothing more than good business to show off the car. Mother and Alice will probably want to be dropped off and picked up at the Lutheran Church. Convince Mother that Alice should have the day off. Say you'll take care of everything that needs to be done for Mother. You know how she hates entertaining, but it's the next step and the proper thing to do. I want more than anything for Karen to stay here and marry me. I don't want her family in Denmark to think we don't have the upbringing to behave properly. Lily Loring will be coming with her, since that's where she's staying. Lily remembers Mother from the old days from way back when she and Lily's mother used to ride together. And Lily always asks about you, Stephen. Just be sure leave Alice off on the way home. It would be awkward if she were there for tea."

Stephen had listened to all of Mark's instructions carefully but now he was puzzled. "What do you mean?"

"You know what I mean. You know how Mother is. Treats Alice like one of the family. Karen isn't going to understand that. She was brought up in Denmark, after all. I know her grandfather was a planter here in Danish times, but that doesn't mean anything to her. As far as Karen is concerned, all colored people are servants."

"Obviously she hasn't been informed of some of our relative's family backgrounds."

"That's why we have to be doubly careful. After all, we're not directly related to the Granard cousins and they are socially acceptable."

"For God's sake, Mark. You're being ridiculous. Great-aunt Cecilia is hardly ancient history. We all knew her and loved her. You're going to deny her existence?"

"Of course not. How could anyone deny the existence of the estate she inherited and the fact that she was light-skinned and beautiful? And that was a different time. We're more careful about choosing whom we marry now, more civilized, much more like the Americans. What are you getting so angry about? I'm just asking for one little favor. After Karen decides she really likes it here, wants to stay here, all these things will be easier to explain. Please help me with this. You know how I feel. You must have felt the same way about Dorothy."

Somewhat surprised, Stephen realized he no longer thought very much about Dorothy but he did feel a great deal of anger about any possible offense to Alice.

"Please, Stephen, it's such a little thing but it could be crucial at this point. You know, Karen spent time at the Royal Palace in Copenhagen, she's used to the best. She means so much to me." Stephen had never seen Mark look so vulnerable and agreed to do what he could to please him without offending Alice.

When Stephen informed the Administrator that he had decided to accept the offer of full-time employment, Captain Warner sighed with relief. "I must confess these are very troubling times for me. It's so hard for me to concentrate on my work when my wife is unhappy. I need someone calculating and analytical to talk to. To pull me back when I start to wander. My wife's obsessed by the thought that our son wants to be called into combat. Well, that's not going to happen, certainly not right away, and it will be a short war I hope. There's no reason why he should be transferred from the naval base in Virginia Beach. The assignment was no special favor. Many of the new graduates from Annapolis are being sent there."

"That should be a comfort to her."

"Well, yes, in a way, except that she's insisting she wants to go visit him and that isn't easy to arrange right now. I've put in a request, but civilian travel is very restricted now. Special permissions are needed. She doesn't understand, she's unwilling to understand and I can just do so much. And I don't blame her. There's a lot of loneliness for women in this life. Hardship, even danger, and at her age, she deserves better."

"I'm sorry, sir. But perhaps, as you say, the best thing is to get to work. Has a code been put in place for incoming dispatches?"

The Administrator was temporarily diverted from the topic of his wife and answered that the code was now in place for urgent communications and slower mail would come in via Saint Thomas via the diplomatic pouch. He warned Stephen that there would surely be a lot of repetition and it would be Stephen's responsibility to sort out what was relevant. "You will stay for lunch, I hope. My wife has a right to complain, but she will complain in private. Americans mustn't whine in public. Bad example for these people. How's your mother, by the way? I heard she had an accident with her leg?"

"She's recovering. She's keeping busy. When I got home last night she was painting a mural up the side of the stairway even though sitting on the stairs must have been pretty uncomfortable."

"Good woman. Hope that Hokansen doctor fellow is able to help her. He did a remarkable job in Panama getting rid of the mosquitoes and treating the fever and the Panamanians never gave him any credit for it. Well, we Americans might as well get used to it. Roads, schools, hospitals, nobody complains about those, but spray a few mosquitoes and all hell breaks loose thanks to the likes of Ralph Henry."

"Should I get started on those dispatches now, sir?"

"Yes. I'm off on a tour of the island in my new automobile. Taking my wife, to get her mind off her troubles. We'll be back for luncheon no later than one-thirty."

Stephen found himself so engrossed in decoding that he did not glance up from the papers until he was informed that someone had come to see him. The "someone" entered without being announced.

"Can't a body just drop into say hello, Mr. Stephen, without some boy sayin' I got to be announced? Just because you don' come to me in de shop no more don' mean you can't greet a body."

"Why, Beulah, I hardly recognized you. You're looking really well."

"It's de clothes, de new clothes, not ol' Beulah dat looks so good. How you like dese shoes? Real American shoes, I just bought dem here in Christiansted. I makin' good money."

"I heard you were supplying your bread to the hospital now."

"I always did, but never so much. And now I get in paid right away. And now dat me grandson's drivin' a delivery cart, I'm sellin' to de Government House as well. You know, I only been to Christiansted town maybe ten, twenty times in me whole life, what wid funerals and such, and now wid ma cart I kin come everyday if I want to. Don' come dat often. Frederiksted's me home. But since I came today and was right here in Government House, I came in to say good mahnin."

"I'm happy you did. And I'm glad you're doing so well. I remember you weren't so cheerful at first, when the Americans came."

"Got two grandsons workin' fo' me in the bakery now, and mah granddaughter-she's got a new baby --she mindin' de shop. I makin' more money than mah son in de sugar factory. Dat's why I keep tellin' dat Ralph Henry to stop the shtupidness he writin' 'bout the Americans treatin' us bad. Dey treatin' us good, Mr. Stephen, and I'm the first one to say so. We got to win dis war, you know."

"I'll report all that to the Administrator. I'm sure he'll be glad to hear that someone thinks the Americans are doing something good for a change. And I like your shoes."

"Dey men's shoes, you know, me foot dat broad from goin' barefoot all me life, but no more chiggers between me toes. And I got me a diet and some medication at de hospital to treat de pressure. I feelin' good. I really like Dr. Sampson even if he does pester Alice Hansen sumptin' awful. He drives her to La Grange, ya know, when she goes to your mudda, lets on like he's makin' doctor visits. Your mother needs two doctors? Dr. Hokansen goes there often enough. And your mudda's doing real well, I hear."

"My mother's doing very well, thanks to Dr. Hokansen. Alice is taking good care of her," Stephen said calmly. He was determined not to reveal that he now suspected gossip to be the real reason for Beulah's visit. "Would you like a cool drink? I'm sure they have something in the kitchen."

"I done had one when I lef' de bread. But I'll be on my way. Stop by mah store. It's all fixed up all pretty. Very, very sanitary, like de hospital."

Stephen was annoyed by his emotional reaction to Beulah's remarks. Nothing could be hidden on this island, he reflected, not among "these people" as Captain Warner called them. He remembered Miranda Muckle's warning about Lieutenant Sampson's possible interest in Alice Hansen, but Stephen had chosen to accept Alice's assurances that it was just nonsense, an irritating interference by Miranda into the personal lives of her young trainees. When Mark told him that Sampson was seriously courting their cousin Dee Dee, Stephen chose to forget the whole thing.

But Beulah's reminder forced him to consider the possibility that Lieutenant Sampson might be pursuing both women and didn't care who knew about it. Stephen was hearing different versions of something unimportant perhaps, exaggerated certainly, and not really his concern. Still, it rankled, the outsider crossing lines that should not be crossed, behaving in a way locals were wary of. An American Naval officer, the Navy itself, would be an ideal object for Ralph Henry's wrath if a young island girl from a respectable family were in any way compromised.

During luncheon Stephen managed to listen politely to Mrs. Warner's complaints about the rigors of island life, yet by the time he reached Frederiksted in the late afternoon he was still unable to transcend his anxiety. He was certainly not in full control of himself when he bumped into Alice on the front balcony as she was preparing to leave his home. She had waited to tell him personally that she would be going to America in a few days.

CHAPTER EIGHT

Stephen rode into Frederiksted town the following morning with his father and brother in the new car although he would have preferred to stay home with his mother to discuss Alice Hansen's imminent departure. But his father insisted that Stephen accompany him in response to a message from Ralph Henry. The newspaper editor wanted to see Stephen right away.

"Are you sure Mother is well enough to be left alone all day?" he asked his father.

Cedric Markham was impatient. "I always see to it that she is well taken care of. The doctor says she is well enough to move around freely and she is hardly alone. We have a housekeeper and a maid and a gardener that she spends most of her time with. Just find out what Ralph Henry wants."

"Maybe he's heard that I'm getting interested in politics," Mark said.

But Ralph Henry had other things on his mind and brought them up immediately after the usual "good-mornings".

"I have a favor to ask," he said.

Stephen, accustomed to being the petitioner, was unprepared for this unusual approach.

"If I can," he said cautiously.

"I have received word that Roger Baldwin will be arriving in a few days and it is my responsibility to entertain him. He is here specifically to talk to me, as the leader of the workers. Frankly, Stephen, my home is a little too humble for the likes of Roger Baldwin. Someday, I'm going to have a big house in Christiansted, someday, but right now...do you think your father could accommodate him in the Markham town house?"

"Why didn't you ask my father?"

"Because I don't think he knows who Roger Baldwin is, and you do. You do, don't you?"

Stephen nodded. Throughout his law school years the activities of Roger Baldwin had been followed with interest by the students at Harvard, many of whom were partisans of the American Civil Liberties Union and its goals. Stephen remembered the discussions and the subsequent prominence Roger Baldwin had achieved among political activists.

"Well, will you?" Ralph Henry was obviously anxious, glancing repeatedly at the pile of papers in front of him and then out the window at the untidy back yard.

"Let me try," Stephen said. "My father is a hospitable man, might even enjoy talking to someone from New England. Perhaps I can do even better. I'll try to arrange a meeting with the Administrator."

"That would be ...fortuitous," Ralph Henry said, impressed enough to choose his words carefully.

"I would be much more likely to bring it off if you wrote a few favorable editorials about the war effort," Stephen said. "It would help back up my arguments and I could then point to something relevant in the newspapers. You say he plans to visit in about a month? You have time." Ralph Henry made no comment, just nodded his head in agreement.

For the first time since he had returned to the Virgin Islands, Stephen felt that he was behaving like a lawyer. His father acquiesced easily, impressed by the fact that Roger Baldwin had been invited to speak at Harvard, and agreed to have the little-used guest room in the Frederiksted town house prepared for an honored visitor. He even offered the use of the Markham's new automobile. The Administrator, somewhat surprised by the request, was also impressed by the Harvard Law School connection but swayed even more by an appeal to official duty. He agreed to a meeting.

"I've heard this man's a rabble-rouser but he's an educated gentleman and I will treat him as such. My guess is that Ralph Henry will be on his best behavior during the visit. Well, well. So Roger Baldwin's coming to our little island to see how we treat the local people. He'll see that we treat everyone with courtesy. Please thank your father for being his host. My wife is not really well enough to have guests at Government House."

Stephen began to appreciate the role of women in social planning when his mother also begged off from any part in the entertaining of Roger Baldwin. She did not care if he stayed at the town house as long as she did not have to be involved, although she agreed that hospitality demanded some sort of informal function for a distinguished guest. Mark came to the rescue.

"Let me ask Karen and Lily to help. Lily is always having parties up at Buelow's Minde and they're lots of fun. You would know if you came to them once in a while," Mark said. "Believe it or not, old man Loring is going to buy a car so Lily can drive him around, so getting to Frederiksted won't be a problem for Lily."

"You should go to the parties, Stephen," his mother interrupted. "You really should enjoy yourself while you're young."

Stephen felt it would be wiser not to admit he had been enjoying himself as long as he could see Alice every day. The thought that that situation was about to change and he really would need some help with the Baldwin visit made Mark's offer agreeable.

"I would appreciate that, if they really want to do it," Stephen said.

"I'm sure they would." Emboldened by this minor success, Mark continued on to his major concern. "When can I bring them to visit you, Mother? I would like Karen to meet you. It's important, or I wouldn't ask."

Kristin Markham looked at her older son carefully, her own expression impossible to interpret. "Soon. I'm feeling a lot better now, though it's been a great disappointment to me to have Alice leave, she's been such a good companion as well as a nurse. I will let you know, Mark. Soon."

Stephen was happy to see his brother, usually so calm and measured in his approach to any change in routine, elated about automobiles, parties, and his mother's willingness to meet the woman he hoped to marry. He also felt a very deep envy. Alice had also been happy and excited as she prepared to leave, inviting him to share her good fortune. He felt like an island of misery surrounded by a calm shining sea of happiness.

"I know it's sudden, my leaving like this," she had replied when Stephen had mentioned his surprise at her abrupt decision. "But everything worked just right. I can get passage on the next ship, Daddy has been asking, you know, about when they could take a few passengers on the freighters. Your mother's leg is better, she's feeling well, and Miranda Muckle said I've learned all I possibly can here at the moment. I've earned my diploma, and she said and to go ahead if Harlem Hospital will accept me. And I have a letter from them saying they will. I'm sad to go in a way, but things may not work out so well again. It's in the stars, don't you think? I'm *supposed* to go now."

Stephen silently cursed the stars but did not want to dampen Alice's good spirits in any way.

"You do plan to come back, don't you?" he asked.

"Oh, yes. After I've finished my training and seen all I want to see up there. I'll miss my family and your mother and you. Mommy half-hopes I'll meet some nice doctor and marry him, but I have orders to bring him back to St. Croix if that happens."

This thought did not make Stephen any happier but he managed to wish her well

and say he hoped to see her again before she left. Alice said she would try, which, as Stephen knew, in Cruzan parlance this meant probably not. His plan now was to dispel his grief through immersing himself in the intricacies of the Jones Act and be able to carry on as usual when he surfaced. He did not want his others to notice how deeply the thought of Alice's imminent departure depressed him. Fortunately, in the distraction offered by preparations for the Baldwin visit, concealment was possible.

This simple exchange of pleasantries about Alice's departure took place in the presence of Kristin Markham, and was comfortably familial. Alice also said that she had requested that no one come down to the ship to see her off.

"You'd be surprised at how many people think they have the right to tell me what to do. It's my parent's business, after all, if they want to allow me to go to America. But no, everybody in the church has an opinion. Some say it's dangerous for a young, black girl up there. Others say it's my duty to stay here and work now that the government has paid for my training and a whole group of church women say I have no business leaving my home and should be thinking about getting married."

"But surely some agree it's a good thing," Kristin Markham said. "For you to go away for more training, to find a life for yourself."

"Just a few. Miranda Muckle for one. After all, she went all the way to Denmark."

Stephen made no comment. Unexpectedly intense sentiments were surfacing. He was not sure how he felt and found that his vocabulary inadequate. He knew that he did not want Alice to go, that her presence had become an important part of his life and that perhaps he had mistaken gratitude for his mother's care for some other more personal need. He was reluctant to admit that for a second time he was being deserted by a woman he cared about and needed. He managed to wish Alice well politely and then left her with his mother as they exchanged addresses. He did not trust himself to be alone with her to say good-bye.

Mark's contentment over the following months exacerbated Stephen's own sorry state. Mark, proud of his family's conveyance, drove off to see Karen and their friends after work during the week, and was absent most of the weekend attending social functions. His mother, feeling better under Dr. Hokansen's prescribed diet, was gardening and painting, leading a more enjoyable life than his own which revolved around analyzing and synthesizing the Jones Act and ancillary government reports, mostly regulations about trade that was non-existent until the war came to an end.

"If you want Lily and Karen to help you with the Roger Baldwin visit, the least you can do is come to the party Lily is giving next Saturday," Mark told him.

Stephen pushed the pile of papers aside wearily. "You're right," he said.

Mark was obviously delighted. "Mother really can't put off a visit from Lily and Karen much longer and if that works out well, the next big party will be an engagement party for us. You will use your influence with Mother, won't you? You do like Karen, don't you?"

Stephen was ashamed to admit to his eager brother that he had never thought very much about Karen one way or another. He had been too involved with his work and island problems to even be curious about the woman who might become his sister-in-law.

"I don't feel that I know her very well," he finally said. "She is certainly very pretty and very pleasant."

"She's more than that. She's beautiful. And Lily's getting better-looking, now that she's lost some weight. She's taken up smoking, you know. It's a secret, her father doesn't know, and she's afraid people would not approve."

Stephen laughed. "Half the old women on the island smoke."

"Not young women from good families. At least, that's what some of the old biddies in church say. But we don't care. We're really quite a modern, free-thinking group, Stephen. We have a lot fun."

All the things that Ralph Henry would say about the privileged youth of the island, remaining deliberately unaware of the serious problems of poverty and disease around them, went through Stephen's mind, but he pushed them aside as he glanced over at the Jones Act lying on his desk. He could not think of a single reason why Mark and his beloved should not be happy and he, Stephen, had work to do.

"I'll tell Mother that Karen is someone worthy of you and she should meet her, if that's what you want," he told his brother and felt guilty when Mark thanked him profusely.

It took several weeks before Kristin Markham could be persuaded. "Mark does not need my permission, or even my approval, to marry. She sounds like a decent young woman and he's obviously made up his mind. I have work I want to finish. My energy is limited. Why are you being so persistent? Why do I have to spend a tedious afternoon with small talk?"

"You know why, Mother," Stephen answered. "Mark wants you to. He's very proper and conventional and marriage is a very serious thing to him."

"Of course it's serious. You're talking to someone who left her homeland and family to get married. I 'm just saying he doesn't have to bring her here."

"Yes," Stephen said, "yes, he does."

Kristin Markham sighed and finally agreed to a meeting the following Sunday afternoon. Alice Hansen would be far out at sea by that time, and Stephen would, to his surprise, be in the good graces of the Administrator.

"I want to congratulate you on getting a favorable editorial out of Ralph Henry for once," he said. "I'm talking about the one on the Jones Act."

"The Jones Act merely recognizes the status quo," Stephen said. "The Danish West Indies have always allowed the ships of all nations to transfer cargo within the island. As I said in my report to you, the Jones Act officially exempts the United

States Virgin Islands from the requirement that only U.S. vessels could be used for transportation between U.S. ports. It merely recognizes the only practice that makes sense."

"I agree. But I feared that Ralph Henry would twist it around to some sort of imperialistic policy. By and large, his editorials have been fairly favorable to the government lately."

Stephen smiled. "It wasn't that difficult. I made a bargain with the devil," he said and told Captain Warner about the promise extracted in return for entertaining Roger Baldwin.

The Administrator looked Stephen up and down approvingly and said, "So you're becoming a diplomat as well as a lawyer."

"Oh, I don't know, sir," Stephen said. "Just a little bit of give and take. A strategy Mark and I developed growing up to keep from upsetting Mother."

"Believe me, that's diplomacy. I know, because it's a skill I lack--I'm too used to giving orders and having them obeyed promptly. I'm fortunate to have you around. By the way, I understand your brother is about to become engaged to that pretty young lady from Denmark. Perhaps you could arrange for them to have luncheon with my wife at Government House someday soon."

When Stephen passed on the invitation, Mark was delighted. It compensated for the fact that Kristin Markham had finally set a date for meeting Karen and Lily, but it was two weeks away.

"She says she wants to wait until her leg is completely better, but it is better, you can see that. The delay is messing up the plans that Lily has for a party a Buelow's Minde. It was going to be an engagement party for us, but she can't wait. One of the Granard cousins in going to England and Lieutenant Sampson is leaving soon…"

"I didn't know Lieutenant Sampson was leaving," Stephen interrupted.

"Everyone knows," Mark replied grumpily. "Nobody knows why, he just said he'd been transferred. It's all off between Dee Dee and him. She broke it off, I think. Anyway, I wish you'd speak to Mother and see if you can't change her mind."

"I'd leave it alone if I were you," Stephen said.

"Well, promise me that you'll come to the Buelow's Minde party. It's the least you can do if you want Karen and Lily to help you with Roger Baldwin's visit."

Prodded by his mother and brother, Stephen agreed to attend the party. As he arrived at the welcome stairway leading up to the ballroom of the separate dwelling where formal gatherings were held, he met Lieutenant Sampson at the foot of the stairs, looking preoccupied but determined. The polite smile with which he greeted Stephen was barely a smile at all. Fortunately, Lily was waiting for them at the top of the stairway so no awkward conversation was necessary.

"I'm glad you arrived together. Now we can start the party and have something to drink. How nice you look, Lieutenant Sampson." Stephen, who had worn his best linen suit, felt somewhat affronted. "Don't pout, Stephen," Lily continued. "I always call *you* my most handsome cousin."

"All of us outdone by our lovely hostess," Lieutenant Sampson said.

"Thank you. Although I'm still too plump. Father accuses me of sipping rum in the afternoons but so does he, and he's not fat. But I've taken up smoking and I have no appetite at all any more. I'll get thin, you'll see. When I make up my mind to do something, I do it. How's your mother, Stephen? Is she better? I heard she might lose her leg."

"Hardly," Stephen said, reminded of the local propensity for exaggeration and gossip. "She's almost completely well. It was just an infected cut. She had good care."

"So I heard. I also heard that you and Lieutenant Sampson both took good care of her caretaker."

Stephen managed to smile as he stifled his annoyance, reminding himself that despite her changed appearance this was the Lily of old, apparently light-hearted and flirtatious, but whose remarks betrayed an undercurrent of bitterness, at least with him.

"My mother is most grateful for Alice Hansen's excellent care," he said quietly.

"We doctors appreciate good nurses," Lieutenant Sampson said icily.

"Oh, come, don't be so serious," Lily said. "I'm just teasing you. You don't think I'm jealous of some poor colored girl, do you? It's your mother's health I care about, Stephen. Well, Karen and I will be seeing her soon. I imagine your parents are happy about Mark marrying a Danish girl. No more marriages between cousins or we'll end up idiots or something. That's true, isn't it, Lieutenant Sampson. You must know. You're a doctor."

"Endogamy is preferable to exogamy," Lieutenant Sampson said.

"He means," Stephen said, noting Lily's perplexity, "that marriage between relatives is better than marriage between races."

"Oh, well, we don't bother ourselves much about that kind of thing here, do we, Stephen? Come along and say hello to Karen. She has done the decorations in the dining room and they're really lovely."

Stephen was impressed by the floral arrangement of hibiscus and bougainvillea, simple local flowers made unusual by the mixture and contrast of colors. *That talent should please Mother, he thought.* Mark was standing with Karen and seemed delighted to see his brother. Rather at a loss for words, Stephen said "I thought we were the first to arrive."

"Mark doesn't count," Lily said. "He's here so often we consider him part of the family. Anyway, he's always been my favorite cousin. You're next, Stephen. At least you used to be, before you went away. And then after you got back, well, we've hardly seen you any more. Perhaps you were too busy with that nurse."

Stephen was about to say that it was the Administrator who kept him busy, but Lily was too fast for him. "There are the Granard cousins. Doesn't Dee Dee look lovely? But then she always does." Lily went off to greet the new arrivals before either Stephen or Lieutenant Sampson could say a word.

For a few moments after her arrival, Dee Dee's loveliness dominated the room. She was wearing pale green and the famous jade necklace, a family heirloom, which matched her eyes so well it seemed predestined for the only daughter with six male siblings. Stephen was struck by the expression on Lieutenant Sampson's face, a mixture of adulation and annoyance.

"No good could have come of it," Sampson said ambiguously. "Twenty years from now, remember what I said. You people live in a state of chaos and don't know it."

Lily came to summon them to the dining hall for the mid-day meal. "Father says to start right away and when he gets hungry he gets bad-tempered.

By now the early afternoon sun was over the horizon and the slanting rays came in the open windows and lit up the glass and silver on the table. Stephen made an effort to memorize the scene to be able to answer his mother's demand for details when he got home. But as the guests took their seats at random in response to Lily's direction to sit where they pleased, a servant closed the shutters to filter out the sunlight. In the dimmer light details were difficult to distinguish so Stephen was free to concentrate on the conversation, which almost immediately turned to politics.

The Granard cousins gathered around Stephen's end of the table. He had seated himself next to Mr. Loring in the hope of hearing some of the old man's remembrances, but the eldest Granard cousin, Douglas Macfarland, began his questioning before any pleasantries could be exchanged. Lieutenant Sampson was at the other end, sitting between Lily and Karen, far enough away so that the separate conversations could not be overheard.

"I hear that you've become the proverbial 'trusted aide' to our naval administrator," Douglas said. "You will keep us poor planters informed as to what's going on, won't you? I've a feeling we're going to need some help."

"The last figures I saw," Stephen said, "showed that the planters were getting richer by the minute. Everything produced, from raw cane to alcohol from rum, has a guaranteed sale. What more do you want?"

"Strange things are happening. You haven't been out to Granard much lately or you'd know that Americans are buying up the plantations that aren't in production."

"And I've heard," his younger brother Cedric added, "that Ralph Henry is buying up small plots in Grove Place with Labor Union money."

"Well, that I did know," Stephen said. "What he's buying has never been good crop land. He plans to build decent dwellings for the workers. A little house, a little plot to grow provisions."

"Well, better that than Americans coming in and buying the best we have, like Lieutenant Hokansen is doing. We've pretty much decided, Stephen, that all of us in the four families must start buying up the bankrupt estates from the government as soon as we get the capital together. We need to know how the Americans are going to handle the sale of land they took over from the Danish Government, the land appropriated for bankruptcy," Douglas said.

Stephen agreed to find out what he could, reasonably certain that neither the American government nor Captain Warner were interested in retaining ownership of land in Saint Croix.

"Good. Do that. You can be of great help to us," Douglas said. He had assumed his usual posture of command as the eldest of the cousins, an attitude that had once amused Stephen but was beginning to annoy him. "The Danes weren't always as open with us as they should have been, you know, and I doubt the Americans will be much better. But as long as our families own most of the land, we'll continue to be in control."

"Don't forget," Donald, a third brother interjected, "that land ownership is no longer required to be able to vote. You told me to remind you of that, Douglas."

"Yes, I did. Because now is a good time to decide which of us is going to run for the Council when that becomes possible," Douglas said.

Silence followed this announcement. Conversation had not impeded lunch being served and eaten. Oscar Loring, who had appeared to be following the discussion with interest, closed his eyes and fell asleep. Lily must have noticed this, Stephen suspected, because at signal from her the servants began to clear the table of food dishes and refill the glasses. Lieutenant Sampson approached Stephen and said he had to get back to the hospital.

"I'll drive back with you," Stephen said. "Speak to Mark about politics," he advised the Macfarland brothers. As Stephen rose from his chair, Douglas extended a restraining hand and Cedric Macfarland interceded quickly.

"Everyone down at the sugar factory says Ralph Henry is going into politics. Is that true? They say the whole Labor Union would vote for him."

"I hope the Americans realize what they have created here," Douglas said. "Imagine having Ralph Henry in the Council."

"The Council has been temporarily suspended. Elections won't be held until the war is over," Stephen said. "Goodbye."

As he turned to follow Lieutenant Sampson, Stephen heard Cedric say "Let's hope it's a long war."

Karen noted their leaving and accompanied them to the top of the stairway. "You didn't used to leave so early, Lieutenant, but I guess I should be grateful you both came at all. I'll be coming down to see you and your mother soon, Stephen. Don't forget."

"I won't. Please tell Mark I left the car for him. The keys are in it."

Lieutenant Sampson took Stephen's arm as they descended the stairway. "Sorry. I'm afraid I drank too much. Not a good idea in this heat. Would you mind driving?"

Stephen hesitated. Mark had instructed him and Stephen felt competent at the wheel of the Markham's car, but he did not consider himself accomplished enough to drive a vehicle belonging to someone else. Without giving Stephen a chance to refuse, however, the doctor climbed into the passenger's seat and put his head back as if to go to sleep. Stephen hoped for silence to concentrate on the shifting of gears but was due for a confession instead.

With his head resting against the seatback and his eyes still closed, Lieutenant Sampson began to speak in a slightly slurred fashion. "I loved that woman. I did, by God. She's a gorgeous woman. And I'm a gentleman. I wanted her to marry me and come back to Virginia. All I asked of her was never to mention her colored grandmother and she refused. Imagine! Refused. Said she loved her granny and would never deny her. I even considered staying here and then--you people, you people. Lieutenant Hokanson did not protest in the least when the Governor in St. Thomas appointed a colored hospital administrator to come over here and supervise our hospital in Saint Croix. A colored man would have outranked me. *I* would have had to abide by *his* decisions on hospital procedure. I told Lieutenant Hokansen this was absolutely unacceptable. I even told Captain Warner, but he declined to interfere. He suggested a transfer if I wanted it. So I took it. I'm a naval officer, after all. I cannot let you people ruin my career. This place will never become civilized. You have no idea of how society should behave. Chaos. That's what you have here. Chaos. "

Stephen said nothing. He had heard about the new hospital administrator and as far as he knew, everyone at the Frederiksted hospital was satisfied with the appointment. Miranda Muckle had made the request. Her duties had doubled since she had a group of probationary nurses to supervise as well as new trainees. Lieutenant Hokansen was seeing more patients daily and had become increasingly involved in his research into the sugar disease. Both welcomed competent help.

Stephen's continued to focus on driving. The road, once they reached the turn at Kingshill about a mile out of Christiansted, was a straight three-mile run to Frederiksted, an easy drive with no other cars on the road. The doctor responsible for the government vehicle eventually fell asleep, still muttering about the chaos in store for the Virgin Islands. Stephen, grateful for the cooling shade of the giant mahogany trees that formed a canopy over the road, was more uneasy about his present task than concerned about the amorphous horrors Lieuenant Sampson was predicting for the future.

CHAPTER NINE

When Kristin Markham, happy and excited, announced at dinner that Lieutenant Hokansen had asked her to illustrate his new book on the medicinal flora of Saint Croix, her sons and husband expressed delighted approval. Her cheeks had color in them for the first time in years, Stephen noted.

Mark seemed particularly pleased. After Kristin Markham retired for the evening, he said to Stephen. "She's in such a good mood. It will make things go well when Karen and Lily come on Sunday for tea, don't you think so?"

Stephen nodded, certain that Mark's judgment was correct. The aura of unhappiness that customarily enveloped his mother had dissipated and her speech had acquired warmth.

Stephen was therefore surprised when he arrived home on Sunday evening, having carefully stayed away during the introductory tea, to find his mother angry and upset.

"What's the matter?" he said alarmed by her pallor. "Did something happen? Were Karen and Lily unable to come? Aren't you feeling well?"

"Oh, they came and I managed to get through it all right. But I'm not feeling well. I don't like either one of those young women. One is a peasant and the other an upstart."

"Mother, surely you're exaggerating…"

"No. I'm not. That girl, Karen, speaks the most atrocious Danish, the language of an uneducated peasant. And Lily! Oh, Stephen, there's nothing of her mother about her, she's her father all over again. Absolutely determined to get what she wants no matter whom she hurts. I can see it in her. Poor Mark. He's so besotted with that Karen girl he can't see straight about anybody or anything."

Stephen, without much conviction, began to defend the girls but his mother interrupted him.

"Stephen, listen to me. You know nothing about Denmark. These farm families don't educate the girls, they're too parsimonious for that. They select one of the daughters who is better-looking than the rest and send her off to do domestic work in the Danish court or for one of the nobility. That way the girls can learn manners, and how to dress and set a table. But they don't ever learn how to speak properly or discuss anything with intelligence. They're trained, but not educated. Karen isn't the sort of woman I would like to have as the mother of my grandchildren. Not someone who can't speak Danish properly."

"But Karen speaks English well."

"That simply hides the fact that she doesn't know her own language. And Lily. All she could talk about was how she was running the plantation for her father and how many horses and cattle they had. She's never read a book. It's all terribly sad. Her mother, Lillian, was so accomplished. She played the piano beautifully and was so charming and beautiful, besides being the best rider on the island. But she chose to marry that Loring creature.. He was just an overseer, you know. Good-looking and all that but once they were married, he treated her like something he owned. And Lily has sunk to her father's level rather than trying to be like her mother. I worry about Mark."

"I'm sure Mark will be a good influence on Karen, and Lily too, for that matter, rather than vice versa."

"I'm not so sure. He doesn't have your background. God knows I missed you when you went to America to study, but I'm glad of it now. It strengthened you. The way illness has strengthened me. Nothing can take what you've learned away from you. But Mark. What does he know except your father's business?"

"It demands a lot of brains and energy to run a business well. And besides, Mark may go into politics."

"That may be a comfort to your father, but not to me. I'm going to bed now." She rose wearily. "I don't feel well."

If Mark had noted his mother's displeasure he did not mention it at their Sunday supper, eaten in relative silence and haste as Mr. Markham had a vestry meeting before the evening services. Stephen hesitated before refusing his brother's invitation to accompany him to a party at the Country Club. Not in the mood for company but later, feeling abandoned in the quiet house, he decided to walk down the road that led past the Hansen plantation. He was tempted to go in and ask what they had heard from Alice but was afraid her parents might think he was being overly familiar. Returning home slowly, he remembered how much his mother enjoyed her conversations with Alice and wondered if this memory affected her reaction to Karen and Lily. Overwhelmed by pervasive loneliness, he had difficulty in going to sleep.

When Lily Loring appeared at his Christiansted office the following morning inviting him to a luncheon she was planning at her home for "...just the four of us, Karen and Mark and you and me, to discuss a few plans..." he accepted. He wanted to get to know Karen better and see for himself if his mother's harsh opinion of the two young women was justified.

Stephen arrived at promptly at noon to find Lily alone. She admitted that she had asked him to come earlier than the others because she did not want to trouble them with her concern. His mother, she told Stephen, had been polite and Mark and Karen were so engrossed in each other they hardly noticed that Kristin Markham had not actually seemed happy about the marriage. She had raised no objections and it was not until after Mr. Markham had joined them to offer his son congratulations that she mentioned to Lily that it would be inconvenient for her to attend her son's wedding.

"Your mother must come. Really she must. You know what people will say if she doesn't."

"What could they possibly say? People know she isn't well, hasn't attended social functions in years."

"You have to be very sick, dying almost, not to go to your son's wedding. And she does go to church, most of the time. People are liable to say anything. That she doesn't like Karen. That she doesn't get along with Father and me. That's so ungrateful of her, since we're giving the reception after the ceremony. She should think about Mark. People might say she's a secret drinker or is losing her mind. You know how people talk."

Stephen silently reflected that Lily was probably right. He pitied her obvious distress. She was twisting her hands nervously and kept pushing her dark blonde hair back from her perspiring neck. When Lily was fatter she had been more placid.

"I'm afraid I don't care much about how people talk. I know Mother doesn't," he finally said.

"Well, it bothers me. Ever since I can remember I've overheard people gossiping about my mother drinking and my father chasing colored women and it's bothered me a lot, I can tell you that. I've always wanted to go away and stay away but Father wouldn't let me. Just that one short summer in Denmark when I met Karen. I enjoyed it so much. But he said I had to come back, to learn how to run the plantation, since he had no sons. No legitimate sons, that is. I had to be right here or he might have willed Buelow's Minde to one of those outside children. All I've ever wanted was respectability." Lily paused and looked at him beseechingly. When Stephen did not comment she continued, "Your mother must come. I know *you* understand, Stephen. You've had problems with your mother like I have had with mine."

"I've never considered my mother a problem, Lily. Never. But just to please you, I will ask her."

When questioned, Kristin Markham denied that she had refused to attend her son's wedding. "I merely said that I found long church services extremely painful, sitting in those hard pews, unable to move. I warned you about Lily, Stephen, how she might exaggerate and distort, just to make trouble, to have everything her own way. I will be at the church service--I'm even having a new dress made--but I expect you to take care of arrangements for the dinner so I'm not too tired to attend."

"What dinner?"

"We will have to have a dinner the evening before the ceremony. It's a customary thing. What would Lily say if the Markham family didn't do that? I will not allow her to make any more trouble. The dinner will have to take place at the town house, of course. Take care of it for me, Stephen, please." Before he could protest, his mother left the room.

Feeling that he had been somehow outmaneuvered by two women, Stephen approached his brother Mark for help. His brother begged Stephen to excuse him from this social responsibility. He had to find a place to live in Christiansted, set up a place of business for the Christiansted branch of Markham and Sons as well as carry on with the daily business. "We're not even going to have a honeymoon trip until after the war is over," Mark said. "Karen wants me to visit her family in Denmark, of course. We need our own house once we are married, even though Lily has invited us to stay on at Buelow's Minde. She's awfully lonely, you know. But Karen wants her own home, and so do I. We've lived at home long enough, you and I."

Stephen was discomfited by the appraising look his brother gave him, which was quickly followed by a compliment. "You did such a good job on the reception after the Transfer ceremonies, Stephen. Do this for me."

A formal reception for the American Navy was an easy task, Stephen reflected, compared to Cruzan dinner for family and friends. Plenty of rum punch and simple crackers and cheese and small sandwiches satisfied the requirements for entertaining the new ruling officialdom. But the so-called Four Families would expect a full dinner and the polo-playing Granard cousins had prodigious appetites. Since the Markhams had not entertained at a family function for so long, everything would be closely observed and severely criticized. Stephen spent a few frantic hours trying to concentrate on his work while he went over in his mind, step by step, the preparations for the Transfer reception and what had taken place there. Suddenly he recalled Beulah's impromptu invitation and her recent visit to his Christiansted office to describe the successful enlargement of her business. Within minutes he was on his way to her bakeshop and was fortunate to find her enjoying a quiet afternoon lull, sitting in a rocker with her shoes off, reading the local paper.

"Why, good afternoon, Master Stephen. So you decided to stop by and see poor ole Beulah," she said as she removed her feet from the balcony rail. "Take a seat over there, me boy. Just watch me plants, don' push dem over de ledge. I'm sittin' here readin' what dat no-good Ralph Henry has to say."

Stephen remembered to wish her a good afternoon before he asked for her help. To his relief, she seemed delighted at the request.

"Of course I can do food for a family party, 'course I can. Real food, too, not those little green and yellow mouthfuls. I can get me grandson to roast a pig and I make the best kallaloo on the island, if I do say so meself."

Stephen felt his anxiety ebbing as Beulah added to the menu, confident now that she would come up with what the wedding guests would enjoy. Not only that, she was happy to be doing it. He had no doubt that her description of the wedding feast would be reported more quickly and accurately than the account in the newspaper.

Stephen also received warm thanks of approbation from his family.

"A good idea, my boy, since we don't have the household help we used to and just getting the town house fixed up properly will be a job in itself. Good thinking," Cedric Markham said.

Praise from his father was so rare that Stephen basked in it. His mother smiled and nodded, her thoughts apparently elsewhere. Mark was overjoyed and agreed that Karen would take care of the invitations. It went so well that Stephen became apprehensive, a feeling that led him to seek out the man who usually caused such a reaction.

"Yes, I have the announcement ready to print," Ralph Henry said. "No need to worry. Everything is taken care of. Lily Loring brought me the whole thing, all written out very carefully. I do not need that young woman to tell me how to spell Danish names. I spent more time in Denmark than she did, and I doubt if *she* could pass a law exam."

Ralph Henry's ill humor restored a sense of normalcy. So too did his reminder that Roger Baldwin would soon be arriving.

"I hear Beulah's doing the wedding dinner. I hope you can arrange something similar for the visit."

"Do you have the date yet?" Stephen asked.

"You know I don't," Henry answered. "We get no definite dates on arrivals these days. But it will be soon."

Ralph Henry was right. The arrival dates for vessels of any kind were no longer specified, even in the coded messages the Administrator received. How effectual this precaution was, no one could judge. Captain Warner often reminded Stephen that no submarines had been sighted in the nearby Caribbean, although in the Frederiksted hospital recuperating patients still watched for them, seated patiently at the windows with a clear view of the sea.

"Best to be safe though," Captain Warner said. "No need to announce arrival dates. When the time comes, these people can work a little faster at the unloading if they want to. How much arrival notice do the laborers need? They're just hanging around the pier anyway and can spot a ship forty miles away with the naked eye."

Despite his success in delegating the actual work of preparation for the Markham dinner, Stephen still had to spend a lot of time attending family festivities. And as a full-time employee of the United States government, Stephen was now required to see that all federal policies were implemented, not just the eradication of the *Aedes Aegypti* and *Anopheles* mosquitoes and the diseases they caused. The final report on mosquito eradication had been approved by the Administrator, sent to Washington and a letter of commendation had been received.

"Thank God the first step is over," Captain Warner said to Stephen. "That was a relatively easy assignment because I knew what to do, how it should be done and an experienced doctor like Hokansen to work with. You did a good job avoiding local opposition and making the Americans look good. What's Ralph Henry saying about the program now?"

"Nothing much," Stephen said. "Which is a good sign. My mother has heard from the servants who heard it in the street that the program cleared up the fleas and bedbugs as well. I doubt that Ralph Henry is going to admit in print that those things were prevalent here, but the people know."

The Administrator nodded his satisfaction, but quickly moved on to the next problem. "All right, now let's get that dam functional and the roads fixed. The war news is better, thank God. Now that the Americans are over there it looks as if it might not last long."

The duration of the war was a personal as well as an official preoccupation with Captain Warner because of his son who, Stephen knew from viewing some semi-official correspondence, was continuing to request an overseas combat assignment. Mrs. Warner mentioned frequently that she was so grateful her son was "…making a significant contribution from his desk in Virginia…" and Stephen was quite sure the Administrator was caught in a struggle between his wife and son. Obviously for Captain Warner the best, but never-to-be-admitted, solution for his family conflict was the cessation of the war.

The longer workday would have been easier if Stephen lived in Christiansted, but now that his brother was leaving the family home such a move had to be postponed. Stephen would soon have exclusive use of the car as Mark had confided that his father had promised him one of his own as a wedding present. Lily's father had ordered one for her, a fact she made known quickly to everyone, Mark said.

"Lily?" Stephen said.

"Don't look so surprised. Women do drive cars, you know. And if Lily can control some of those spirited horses she has, a car will be easy for her. It seems the old man looks forward to the idea of being driven around like the old patriarch he is and he likes to tell her what to do. I don't envy her the job of being his chauffeur. On the other hand, he sleeps most of the afternoon, so then she'll have the car for herself."

The wedding date was the 21st of June, *Hans Aften Day* in the Danish tradition, just another excuse for a party, Kristin Markham always said, and a stupid one at that. "It never made much sense, even in Denmark," she said. "Of course we were all sun worshippers after that long winter and gloomy spring. But burning witches and all that medieval nonsense, I never had much use for it, even as a child. My grandfather was a Lutheran pastor and we were taught better. And here, God knows, we get too much sun. Why make a big fuss over the longest day of the year?"

Stephen soon discovered that there was to be no way out of the social engagements for him. His mother was obviously feeling better, quite happy with her new assignments as an illustrator, and Lily needed him, she said, to escort her to the parties in and around Frederiksted where she did not feel as comfortable as she did at Buelow's Minde where her reign as the foremost hostess had long been accepted. Although the long workdays and hot summer weather made Stephen long for quiet evenings in the cool of the La Grange great house, he found himself attending parties with Lily and Karen and Mark. He comforted himself with the thought that all the social activity would be over as soon as the wedding took place.

Then word came through, simultaneously it appeared, to both the Administrator and Ralph Henry, that Roger Baldwin would be arriving on or about the Fourth of July, and that some sort of commemorative event should be planned for that time as well, since the islands were now part of the United States and should share its national holiday.. Stephen himself wrote the editorial explaining the history of the Fourth of July, feeling like a schoolteacher as he did so, and asked Ralph Henry to publish it on the appropriate date.

Ralph Henry read the one-page presentation in silence, started to speak several times, became silent, swallowed hard. Under ordinary circumstances there would have been an argument, but in light of the need for Stephen's help during the visit of Roger Baldwin, it appeared that concession was the newspaper editor's approach.

"All right," he said. "I'll print it. But I'm going to write my own description of our real holiday, July 3rd, our Independence Day."

The Administrator considered this solution an equitable one, and congratulated Stephen on his adroit handling of what might have been a difficult situation, the first insistence on a public display of changed allegiance from Denmark to the United States. Stephen's main worry now was that

Mark's wedding be the joyous occasion his brother was looking forward to.

To Stephen's great relief the dinner party was a success. The guests demonstrated their approval of the food by eating enormous quantities, and the more they ate, the more Beulah beamed. "If they don' wan' the left-overs, Mister Stephen, I got a whole passel of family just waiting for a taste," she said.

"Take it, take it, and enjoy," Stephen said grateful that the guests were leaving early, confident that there would be another feast on the following day at Buelow's Minde after the wedding.

The church ceremony proceeded in perfect order and solemnity. From where he stood at the altar at his brother's side, Stephen had a good view of his parents in the front row, his father in the black "funeral suit", not worn since Transfer Day, and his mother resplendent in her new dress. The design was the same loosely flowing style she always wore, but of a diaphanous material the same shade as her gleaming white-blonde hair. As soon as the ceremony was over, Stephen made his way quickly toward her to thank her for coming, but Lily stopped him.

"It was a lovely service, wasn't it?" she said, putting her hand on his arm and looking up into his eyes.

"Yes, it was," he answered.

"You looked so handsome at the altar, Stephen. You and Mark. Him so dark and you so fair, yet so obviously brothers. And Karen looked beautiful, didn't she?"

"Yes," Stephen said. "Yes, she did."

"And your mother," Lily added, turning her gaze toward the Markhams. "How clever of her to wear white. Quite a rival to the bride, isn't she?"

"Mother always wears white," Stephen protested to Lily's back as she moved off to usher Karen and Mark into the Markham family car. Cedric Markham was deep in conversation with the Administrator so Stephen accompanied his mother home in the carriage. She urged him to go on to the reception confessing that she was too tired to talk.

"Don't linger here," she said to Stephen. "I'm perfectly all right, I just want to be alone and quiet for a while. Be sure Lily sees you and do everything you're supposed to do. I don't want any criticisms from that young woman."

"Lily said you looked lovely," Stephen said, telling himself he was not being hypocritical.

"She did?" Kristin Markham looked skeptical. "Well, tell me all about the party when you get back."

At Buelow's Minde Lily was too busy being hostess to talk to him and after the perfunctory toast to his brother, Stephen prepared to leave. He took a good look around so he could report the details to his mother, noted that the Administrator had arrived, and hoped that the dark clouds forming off the south shore would not, for a few hours at least, produce a torrential rain. A shower *after* the outdoor festivities in the carefully tended garden would be welcomed. The hills to the east were already brown-tinged, camouflaged by the flamboyants, full-blossomed and distracting the casual observer from the portents of drought. A scratchy band arrived to play dance music on their primitive instruments and guests began to move inside to the ballroom. Stephen walked down to the carriage house. No one noticed when he drove away.

CHAPTER TEN

The Baldwin visit was delayed several times because of his other commitments and by the time he finally arrived in early September plans had been repeatedly changed.

The Fourth of July celebration, although much discussed, ended up being a simple affair, a proclamation from Government House in St. Thomas proclaiming the holiday coupled with an announcement that the Americans were still fighting for democracy and freedom.

"Indeed we, the people of the Virgin Islands, still are," Ralph Henry announced in his editorial describing the history of Emancipation Day. And then, alluding to the Roger Baldwin visit, "…and soon all the world will know of our struggle against economic slavery and political oppression…"

This last observation was due to the fact that Roger Baldwin had informed the labor leader that he would be bringing with him six journalists to report on the working conditions on Saint Croix. Cedric Markham now knew who Roger Baldwin was and what he represented and requested to be included in the preparations for the visit.

"I want to be sure that people in America get a fair picture of how we live in the Virgin Islands," he said.

Familiar with the power of newspapers, Stephen understood his father's concerns and so did the Administrator. He
said he would be glad of Cedric Markham's help.

"Since it's a larger party than we expected, the government will have to put them up at the Pentheny Hotel in
Christiansted. That may make things a bit easier as far as
entertaining at Government House is concerned."

"Whatever I can do to help, sir," Stephen said, noticing
that the Administrator was not speaking in his usual decisive
way.

"I know I can count on you to handle this, you have
proven to be a skillful mediator. My wife does not feel comfortable entertaining colored people and I never interfere
with her social arrangements. Perhaps you could arrange for
a separate luncheon for Ralph Henry and the journalists at
the hotel while we entertain Roger Baldwin at Government
House."

Stephen hesitated, but just for a moment, realizing
regretfully that this was probably the best way to handle the
situation. His father, also reluctant, agreed with the compromise. Cedric Markham would be invited to join Roger
Baldwin for the official luncheon with the Administrator and
his wife while Stephen, Ralph Henry and the journalists ate
at the Pentheny Hotel. The decision was based, Stephen realized, not on any matter of principle but uncertainty as to how
the Administrator's wife would behave.

Cedric Markham suggested that he and Ralph Henry,
both familiar with the island, decide upon the route to be
followed by the motorcade of two automobiles that would
convey Roger Baldwin from the pier in Fredriksted to
Government House in Christiansted. Stephen acquiesced,
saying only that he would like Lieutenant Hokansen to be

added to the official party to describe first-hand how the mosquito eradication campaign had benefited worker and planter alike.

The ship arrived during the night but a naval launch brought the official party into the dock promptly at eight o'clock. In accordance with the Administrator's wishes, Stephen was at the dock to escort them to the assigned automobiles. The tall, patrician-looking Baldwin, wearing a white linen suit and a wide-brimmed panama hat over his silvery gray hair greeted Stephen with an unexpected smile of recognition.

"So you're Stephen Markham. I'm happy to have met you so soon. I have a message for you from a friend of yours in Boston. Dorothy Kingsley. She asked me to look you up."

"Dorothy!" Stephen could not control his surprise. "I haven't heard from her in some time. How is she?"

"Very well. Very well. She is working as the Acquisitions Director of the Museum of Fine Arts and I am on the Board. Most attractive young lady. And very intelligent. Engaged to one of my godsons. She has helped me with my purchases. I'm a collector, you now. A very modest one, but I admit it, collecting modern art is my weakness."

"Then you might like to see the collection of Dr. Hokansen's paintings. He's waiting for you over there in the automobile."

"An automobile. Well, that is a pleasant surprise. Somehow I didn't expect such amenities down here. Miss Kingsley, well, she led me to expect something more primitive. But, of course, with the Navy here...that brought about many changes, I suppose."

"Yes, indeed, sir," Stephen said, relieved when Ralph Henry had stepped forward to greet the distinguished guest promising to meet up with him later in the day at the hospital inspection tour. After the usual exchange of pleasantries, the tall, patrician-looking Baldwin, Cedric Markham and Lieutenant Hokansen rode off in the first car with a military driver and Stephen, and the six journalists crowded into the second one. Stephen explained to the pale, perspiring young men that he would point out points of interests as they drove but would prefer that they ask questions later at the luncheon so he could concentrate on the driving.

As they drove through Frederiksted town, he avoided, without comment, stray horses, lazy dogs, runaway cows and careless chickens. His thoughts were still on Dorothy and the news she was engaged to, without doubt, a proper Bostonian. Only a request from his passengers to stop for a moment so they could remove their jackets and ties brought him back to reality.

Beulah Heyliger was standing in front of her bake shop, smiling and waving, when they passed a few minutes later. Stephen was relieved that the journalists followed his example and waved back. As he followed the lead car he did his best to remember the descriptions is father had rehearsed. Estate Two Brothers was once a leading sugar producer and Estate Smithfield was named for a London suburb. Once they made the sharp left turn to Centerline Road, Stephen announced it was now a straight road to Christiansted with plantations on either side. Workers could be seen in the distance in the fields, but were too far away to be closely observed. Stephen lapsed into silence hoping the journalists would be content for a while with their own observations of cane-fields and mahogany trees.

The earlier glimpse of Roger Baldwin, a tall man in an immaculate white linen suit, had not conformed to Stephen's idea of a man often described as a "dangerous radical". But then Ralph Henry, formal, polite and dignified hardly looked like a man who lived and breathed controversy. Stephen had chosen to wear a guayabera, the decorated long-sleeved cool white shirt introduced by the Puerto Ricans, and was gratified by the envious looks of the journalists.

He occasionally pointed out schoolhouses, fruit gardens, and the once-famous stable of the early Governor Sobotker. He paused at the sugar factory at Estate Bethlehem when the other car did, saying he would take them on a tour of it later if they so wished and give them any information they wanted on the working conditions and the machinery. Stephen was forced to slow down as the lead car paused at the Catholic chapel and Midlands Lutheran Church. Certain that his father was explaining the local tradition of religious tolerance, Stephen offered his own version.

"It wasn't easy to find colonists in the early days," he said, hoping the journalists would take note of his conclusion. "Many came here to escape religious persecution and tolerance has become part of our tradition." He noticed that two of the men scribbled down his remarks but aside from that there was silence until they reached the hotel, an old Victorian-style building up the street from Government House, long converted from private residence to semi-official guest house for important visitors. The food was reputed to the best on the island and to Stephen's taste it was. All the reporters ate heartily, discussing the politically neutral topic of food until the meal was finished. Then Ralph Henry took over the meeting.

Discussing their respective luncheons that evening at dinner, Stephen and his father realized that two very different aspects of the island had been presented.

"Mrs. Warner was very charming," Cedric Markham reported. "She asked us to say grace before we ate saying that she hoped all on the island would some day eat as well as we were about to do. The Administrator allowed Lieutenant Hokansen to do most of the talking. He is a very knowledgeable man and could speak with great conviction about how well the mosquito eradication plan had been carried out benefiting all the residents. He spoke very highly of you, Stephen."

"What did you think of Roger Baldwin?" Stephen asked.

"Very distinguished-looking, impressive, soft-spoken, as men like that often are. But a restless soul. Almost tormented, I would say. I could sense it. A man of little faith, I would say, does not understand that we can do little more than obey God's will. Believes men should do more to help themselves and others, change the world, that sort of thing. However, I think we convinced him that things were not too bad here and had improved under naval rule. I do not think we have much to fear from his report."

Stephen was not so sure. He had watched Ralph Henry manipulate six attentive reporters, two from Boston, three from New York and one from Philadelphia in such a manner that their questions elicited the information labor unions everywhere wanted to hear. That wages of a few dollars a week were inadequate, the housing conditions atrocious and medical care unavailable except for those few workers who lived within walking distance of the hospital in town. Soon the plight of laborers in the United States Virgin Islands would be common knowledge in the leading cities of the northeast.

By the time the entourage was deposited at the ship the next afternoon for the trip to Saint Thomas, Stephen knew that the Administrator's decision to exclude Ralph Henry from the official luncheon at Govenrment House had been a serious mistake. It had given him free access to the reporters for several crucial hours. Stephen could achieve compromise with the editor about what to print locally but he had no control over what the American papers were going to publish. As a result the mainland newspapers could present the labor leader's version of life in Saint Croix without attribution or denial.

It was almost noon before the ship sailed for Saint Thomas so Stephen drove to Estate La Grange to join his mother for lunch before returning to Christiansted. She cleared a space for him to be served his food on the large dining room table almost entirely covered with pages of manuscripts and illustrations, then looked up at him with a warm smile of greeting.

The atmosphere of the room had changed and it took Stephen a few minutes to identify the cause before he dutifully kissed his mother's cheek

"You're looking well. I like your new painting. Whatever did you do with Grandfather's portrait?"

"It's so nice to see you. Lunch is just the usual cabbage soup, I'm afraid. I do feel much better. I'm able to work for a full morning now. This room is much more comforting and cheerful, don't you think, now that your Grandfather's portrait is hanging in your father's bedroom where it belongs, and the one Dr. Hokansen gave me is over the sideboard in my dining room."

"It does improve the room," Stephen said. "What did Father say? And I thought Dr. Hokansen said he would never sell any of those paintings."

"Your father didn't even notice. And I didn't buy it, of course. It's a gift. For the work I've been doing. I wouldn't take any money. A true artist doesn't work for money."

"Of course not," Stephen agreed, sharing his mother's contentment.

"He did sell one, though, to that Roger Baldwin. He offered Dr. Hokansen so much money and promised it would be exhibited at some museum in Boston. Evidently the artist, some Frenchman Dr. Hokansen treated for fever in Panama, died recently at some little island in the South Pacific and his paintings have become very valuable. But you don't look happy," his mother observed, looking steadily into his eyes. "What's the matter? I heard the luncheon at Government House yesterday went well. And Mark told me that the girls prepared a lovely breakfast for the reporters at the Country Club this morning before they left. They didn't invite Ralph Henry, how could they, and Roger Baldwin spent the morning with him. But Dr. Hokansen said that Roger Baldwin seemed impressed by what the naval administration had done to improve public health."

"The journalists heard a different story, I'm afraid, from Ralph Henry. The Americans are going to read stories about most people here being underpaid and exploited, so much so that they suffer from malnutrition."

"Well, at least we're not being invaded by warring armies. I have something to make you happy. Over there on the sideboard is a letter for you from Alice Hansen. I got one too. She's coming back."

"What!" Stephen could not control the exclamation that escaped his lips nor the pounding of his heart. "Why? What happened?"

"I'm sure it's all there in the letter," his mother said. "What she said in her letter to me was that she had been offered a better job down here."

Stephen sat down to read the letter while his mother silently arranged and re-arranged pages of texts and illustrative drawings of tropical plants. He re-read the letter several times and put it down only when his mother reminded him his soup had been served and was getting cold.

"Well, what did she tell *you*?" his mother asked. "She simply told me that she had been offered a position with a medical research facility about to be set up in Saint John and would be coming back soon. Not exactly when, just soon."

Alice had said a lot more than that, but he chose his words carefully in recapitulating part of the letter for his mother. The Rockefeller University, a research institution, was planning to set up a laboratory in neighboring St. John to try to isolate the causes of the influenza epidemic that was rapidly spreading throughout the United States and decimating the troops with severe illness and death. As a medically trained native of the Virgin Islands, Alice had been offered a job with the research team as a laboratory worker.

"She says she has always wanted to work in medical research, ever since she took some classes here taught by Dr. Hokansen. Because of the epidemic, classes at Harlem Hospital have been suspended so the nurse probationers could work in the wards. All of the beds are full in all the hospitals. Alice is glad to be of help but feels she is not getting the scientific training she went up there for and could do more elsewhere, right in her own home. After all, she saw what Dr. Hokansen accomplished," Stephen said.

"Maybe she just wants to come home," Kristin Markham said, pushing her soup plate aside to carefully examine one of her drawings.

"That too," Stephen agreed. He did not tell his mother more of what Alice had said. He wanted to read it over again and try to read between the lines. Alice was trying to tell him something important, he felt sure of that, but was afraid he might misinterpret what she had written. "Why didn't you tell me how colored people were treated in New York?" Alice wrote. "You lived in Boston. You must have known. If I left Harlem I was treated like a pariah. And then the white people would come up to visit the jazz clubs and treated us as mere performers for their pleasure. It was humiliating. If it hadn't been for my memories of Saint Croix I would have hated all white people. I almost did."

But then, Alice explained, just as she reached that point of bitterness, she had been asked to come to the Rockefeller University for an interview. There she had been treated with kindness and courtesy and offered a position she would have dreamed about if she had known such things existed. "I'm not sure what I think or how I feel right now," she wrote. "Illness is everywhere. As far as I can tell, what these white people at the Institute want to do-- and only they are capable of doing it--, is the only hope for all of us. All the talk is of war and an epidemic that is beyond control. I want to work with people who are helping people and not to hate anyone and perhaps I can do that back home in the Virgin Islands. I just know I want to be with people I love and trust and I want this job more than anything I can think of. Maybe I can be of some help to the people who have helped me and are trying to help others. That's the main reason I wanted to become a nurse."

"She says she has been working very hard because of an influenza epidemic," Stephen said, trying to sound non-committal while he wondered if he was one of the people Alice loved and wanted to be with.

"That reminds me," his mother said. "Dr. Hokansen says he would like to talk to you about some new treatment for the sugar disease."

"Why?" Stephen asked reflecting on Alice's use of the phrase "…love and trust…".

"I would like to try it, that's why. He feels he should talk to someone in the family instead of just me because there may be side effects."

"But Father…"

"Your father wants no part of the decision. I think he feels I could be cured by prayer. And Mark has his own concerns. Please Stephen."

"All right," Stephen said, transferring his attention to his mother. She certainly looked better, perhaps did not need to be part of an experiment. If prayer was not the cure his father believed it to be, perhaps art was.

"I certainly look forward to seeing Alice again," his mother said. "I'm sorry it didn't work out for her in New York, but obviously this is where she was meant to be, close by in Saint John. I hope you don't let her get away again."

CHAPTER ELEVEN

Stephen welcomed a rainy Sunday afternoon to spend some time away from Mark's new-found domesticity. It had become routine to stop by the new branch of Markham and Sons in Christiansted after he left Government House to see how Mark was doing and increasingly difficult to refuse dinner invitations. He enjoyed the food--Karen was a good cook--but was discomfited by the growing intimacy that was, he felt, being forced upon him by Lily with encouragement from his brother and sister-in-law.

The rain removed any obligation to go to Granard. His mother, forced into idleness by her husband's dictum against work on Sunday, was sitting in the rocking chair by the window, a book open in her lap as she gazed out at the large mango tree that shaded the courtyard. She seemed delighted with his decision to remain at home.

"You've been neglecting me."

"You haven't even missed me, you've been so busy," Stephen said.

"It's true. I have been busy. And I enjoy it so. Dr. Hokansen is so appreciative. Tell me, how is Mark? What does his home look like?"

Stephen described in some detail the new hardware store in the old, now restored, building with its elegant stone arches, "...too nice for a store..." and the little house on the old Shoys plantation just east of town, tastefully furnished with Lily's help. He commented on Mark's ambition to expand into a car dealership that would make him rich.

"He's pretty obsessed with cars," Stephen said, concluding his description.

Kristin Markham laughed. "When I was newly married we were that way about horses. Lillian, Mary Ramlov and I used to say we cared more about our horses than our husbands. That was before we had any children, of course. We really enjoyed riding around the island, going to the beaches. Good thing we did because the good times didn't last. Lillian got pregnant, and was never well after that. And then Mary died so suddenly, of fever. Poor Peter Ramlov. He took it very hard. A doctor and he couldn't save his own wife. I think it would have been the end of him if it hadn't been for Miranda Muckle. She got him back to his work and wanting to live again. Not that he ever showed her any gratitude."

"What do you mean? I always thought they've always worked together so well."

"Well, they were both very professional and I suppose that after a while they became friends. She was in love with him, of course, but even when he became a widower he didn't seem to notice. Still, she was a young nurse and he depended on her so much. The Danish nursing sisters thought so highly of her, and we all thought he would marry her eventually. Then two old aunts visited him from Denmark and told him such a marriage was unsuitable, he wouldn't get his inheritance, something like that, and he stayed away from her until the old aunts left. The next thing we knew Miranda was off to Denmark to study. We heard she had a love affair there; maybe it was just gossip, I don't know. When she came

- 154 -

back she made it quite clear she wanted nothing to do with Peter Ramlov Nothing personal, that is. She has her work, of course, and her relatives. And there he is, a lonely old man. Serves him right, for ignoring her that way."

Stephen was about to ask more questions aiming for exactness and precision but his mother abruptly changed the subject. "Just listen to that rain. I could sit here and listen to it all day. It's like music. You can practically hear it gurgling into the cistern."

From experience Stephen knew his mother had said her final word on the subject of Miranda Muckle and was aware that the story of Dr. Ramlov would not have been told unless it had special relevance to his own situation. He had long ago learned that when his mother repeated what on the surface seemed to be frivolous gossip she was talking in parables. It was one of the reasons he enjoyed talking to her.

"I'm thinking of taking a trip to St. John," he said. "I haven't been there since father took us once years ago when they consecrated a new chapel. When the Administrator leaves--he says he is going to retire as soon as the war is over--it might be a good idea to set up my law practice in Saint John. I've done what Father wanted. Ralph Henry hasn't criticized the Americans in months. I've worked for the government long enough. I want my own business. Like Mark. "

His mother smiled and nodded her head. "If and when you go be sure you come and tell me exactly what it is like."

Stephen's discontent with the status quo was its lack of excitement. The problem of a good water supply was being ably handled by the naval engineers and no one quarreled with an administration about to provide them with much needed water. Ralph Henry even applauded the work.

Local editorial criticism was superfluous. Stateside newspapers, particularly one in Philadelphia, had published articles on the dire conditions in the American West Indian territories. All Ralph Henry had to do was print excerpts from them. But it was a situation beyond Stephen's influence and he found the infrequent advice he was asked for from Captain Warner, increasingly occupied with the war in Europe, insufficient to produce a sense of accomplishment.

"You should get married," Mark said, apparently sensing his brother's discontent.

"Is that your solution for everything?" Stephen asked, noting that his brother was putting on weight.

"Be practical. Lily will inherit valuable property, she's an attractive woman, and she obviously fancies you. Don't look at me like that. All right. I'll mind my own business, but just remember what I said."

The following week the Administrator suggested that Stephen leave work early as he had received word from two of the naval engineers that the centerline road which connected the two towns was in danger of washing out in one or two locations. There had been three days of steady rain and the gravel-topped road had held up well except where ancient guts were being transmuted into the small streams that they had once been in days that only the old people could remember. When Stephen stopped by the new store to tell Mark he could not make dinner that evening, his brother objected.

"I've asked our cousin Douglas to come. He wants to talk to you about something. And if the road is getting bad, you'll be stuck in Frederiksted for days. The best thing is to stay with us at Shoys. We've finally furnished the guest room so you'll even have a bed. I'll send a message down to Mother with one of the workman who's leaving now on horseback. Don't worry about him. The horses know the roads."

Stephen hesitated long enough for Mark to continue. "You wouldn't want anything to happen to Father's car."

"No. Of course not. Well, thank you, Mark."

The road out to Shoys did not have a coating of gravel and the mud had turned into a slippery ooze. But by the time they reached the house the rain had stopped and the weather suddenly cleared. If the dry, brisk breeze continued he might still make it back to Frederiksted, a thought which became a fervent hope when he saw two other cars parked near the house. He was certain one belonged to Lily--she had been announcing to everyone that her father had ordered a car-- and probably the other one belonged to his cousin Cedric, he namesake and godson of Cedric Markham. The cars were identical; evidently a new shipment had arrived.

"Beautiful, aren't they?" Mark said.

Stephen didn't think so, but he nodded his head in agreement. The models were black like his, but slightly different, in a way he would not readily identify.

"Ceddy is bringing an acquaintance, actually he's the dealer, from Puerto Rico. Let's get inside in case it starts to rain again. Ceddy can tell you what they have in mind."

Of all the Granard cousins, Cedric was Stephen's favorite. He was the youngest of the siblings, not as strikingly handsome as his brothers, a little shorter and stockier, fairer of skin with sandy rather than jet black hair. He was not as good a polo player as his brothers and begged off when a good substitute could be found. For this reason Stephen had talked to him more often at the family gatherings and guessed that Cedric's ambitions to start a business of his own was simply a manifestation of sibling rivalry. The slightly-built man with him was dressed in a dark suit, tense and business-like, pale-skinned with restless eyes. He walked around the room sipping a drink, sometimes passing in front of and obscuring another man in the corner. When he emerged to shake hands he appeared healthy and virile, content to be immobile and silent, hoarding his obvious strength. He looked familiar to Stephen and recognition showed in the man's dark eyes as he nodded in greeting.

"And this is Ramón," said Lily after kissing Stephen on the cheek by way of greeting. "You know him, Stephen. He trains father's horses. And he also knows how to drive a car. He is teaching me."

With this clue to identity, Stephen remembered Ramón. They had often exchanged greetings when he had stabled his horse, but he could not recall seeing Ramón at any of the luncheons or dinners at Buelow's Minde. Evidently, in Lily's eyes, the ability to drive a car improved social status and Ramón was now worthy of joining other guests at the dinner table.

While the usually calm Mark, whose customary posture was sitting relaxed in a planter's chair once the workday was done, nervously sought out half-emptied glasses to fill with more rum swizzles, Ceddy quickly came to the point. His matter-of-fact approach endeared him to Stephen who was tired, hungry and chilled from the rain.

He had decided, Ceddy said, to devote his time and family money to buying some of the estates the federal government had acquired through bankruptcy and was anxious to sell.

"Mr. Stanton here is my first customer. He wants that old plot on Number Two Company Street in Christiansted. Number One has already been sold to your friend Ralph Henry. You didn't know? You two are so close, I thought he would have told you. A group of Virgin Islanders in New York City sent him money to buy that old mansion for union headquarters. Mr. Stanton here wants to put up an office building. That's why we need you, Stephen, we need you to handle the legal details."

Stephen hesitated briefly but decided to be as terse as his cousin. "I am considering setting up a law office in Saint John."

"Oh, Stephen, really," Lily interrupted. "Why don't you stop following that poor woman around? She obviously has enough good sense to know you can't possibly be serious about her. Don't listen to him, Ceddy. He won't settle in St. John. His mother will see to that."

Stephen stared at Lily, then looked over at his brother Mark. Mark looked as surprised as Stephen felt. Lily laughed at their consternation, then explained the source of her knowledge.

"I asked Miranda Muckle to recommend a nurse for my father, he's gotten much weaker you know, he really can't get around without Ramón's help, and she told me that Alice Hansen was coming back soon and was a wonderful nurse, your mother could recommend her. Then Miranda sent me a message yesterday that Alice was going to be working at some new medical facility in Saint John. "

At loss for words Stephen said, "I always had the impression that you had no use for Alice Hansen."

"Don't be stupid. If she's a competent nurse, I'll hire her, as long as she remembers her place and follows my orders. But obviously she has other ideas. But I don't like to see you make a fool of yourself chasing some half-breed around."

"Shall we have dinner?" Karen asked. "Hannah has it all ready."

"Let's sit down," Mark said. "Karen worked hard on this dinner. All day."

"Why waste your time cooking when you can get servants, Karen? Surely your husband can afford some kitchen help for you. Ramón, check the weather. Is it safe to stay for a while?"

Ramón strode to the door. "I think we'd better go," he said. "This may turn into a hurricane and the horses get nervous. I want to check on the stables."

"Well, good-bye then. Sorry about your dinner, Karen, but can't take chances with the horses, nor my new motor car. You'd better drive, Ramón."

Without further comment, she swept from the room followed by Ramón. Everyone was silent and immobile until Mark repeated, "Let's sit down, shall we?"

During the delicious dinner of roast pork and spiced red cabbage, Mark visibly relaxed, enjoying the praise his wife received for her cooking. The conversation centered around the anticipated growth of automobile sales and land transfers all of which, Stephen quickly realized, would demand at least a basic knowledge of contract law.

The breakfast Karen prepared for him the following morning was as good as the dinner and as he drove to his office at Government House Stephen felt disloyal comparing it to the spartan fare at Estate La Grange.

The Administrator welcomed him with a sigh of relief. "So you spent the night at your brother's. I was worried about your trip home yesterday evening and didn't expect to see you this morning. But now that you're here, please drive around the island and see if there has been any significant damage to the roads from the rain. I was going to have the engineers check the culverts and dams, but you can do it much more rapidly. Take the day, if that much time is necessary to do a thorough job. Report back to me tomorrow."

Stephen dutifully drove off, noting that the waters of the harbor were murky and brown. Some of the impacted gravel had washed off the main road but it was relatively free of ruts so driving was effortless. The conversation of the previous evening still echoed in his brain and going west rather than east in the morning created the sensation of a reversed universe. It was an effort to subdue such fanciful, even irrational, thoughts in order to take mental notes of the road conditions.

He noticed that several large fields near town had been cleared allowing a run-off of top soil, but were free of any signs of newly planted cane. This impersonal observation evoked an unusual emotional response; instead of being analytical, he was covetous. He found himself appraising possible building sites, checking the efficiency of the culverts that prevented customary flooding and noting that the mahogany trees had lost very few limbs and protective foliage. He began to calculate where, on a particularly attractive lot, a house could be built to take advantage of trade winds and sea views. He admitted to himself, with an element of surprise, that he wanted a home like Mark's, his own home, filled with a certain amount of wholesome noise, disputatious conversation and the aroma of good cooking. He stopped the car at the first mud-free roadside spot he saw and looked around, telling himself that it was ridiculous to become an irrational thinker as the result of a few good meals.

Nevertheless, it was an effort to return to careful appraisal, so in order to focus his attention he chose the more hazardous route to Frederiksted, Mahogany Road through the rain forest. The engineers did a good job, he thought, driving through the area that customarily received the heaviest rain. Guts on both sides contained the rushing brown water, the small bridges held firm and only a few puddles had collected in the road itself. Although sodden liana vines were hanging low from the trees and strewn about in the mud like somnolent snakes, the way was navigable. He proceeded with caution, an attitude acquired in boyhood from the many times he had ridden through the rain forest on horseback, always mindful that after a heavy rain a misstep into a water-filled hole could break a horse's leg.

Nearing Frederiksted town, he passed the half-hidden path that Alice had shown him the day she led him up to the big dam in the hills. The dam must be filled to overflowing now, its waters constrained and directed by the carefully constructed aqueducts Stephen himself had recommended. These more recent, definitely more poignant, memories distracted him once again. He had been so tempted to swim in the dam the day he and Alice, hot and perspiring from the uphill climb, had sat looking at their green, ghostlike reflections in the cool, still water. Alice had refused to join him, and he had resisted the temptation to plunge in. That unrequited impulse now returned, apparently fomented by the intense longing to see Alice again. Stephen forgot the slippery road and rushing guts and began to drive more rapidly, slowing down only when he skidded dangerously close to an embankment. He was desperate to get home and find out if his mother had received any news of Alice's arrival.

Kristin Markham looked so calm when he saw her through the window, seated by the dining room table, positioned so that the weak sunlight gleamed on her silver-gold hair and illumined the pages spread out before her. She looked up at him with her familiar warm smile as he entered.

"So tell me, how was everything?"

"The rain was very heavy, so heavy it didn't seem wise to drive home in the dark. But the roads held up well."

His mother put down her pencil and sighed with impatience. "I know it rained. The roof still leaks and your father had the servants running around putting pails everywhere. He's down at the store now to check on whether any leaks damaged the merchandise. I don't want to hear about the rain. What I want to know is what Mark's house is like and how that wife of his, Karen, is taking care of him."

Stephen did his best to describe the house, the furniture and the food in a casual but not too enthusiastic manner, yet trying to make it appear that all was going well. He refrained from describing just how happy Mark looked and how good the food had tasted, nor did he refer to Lily's brief presence. His mother seemed satisfied, even a little disappointed, and without further comment, picked up the pencil. After a few strokes she said, "Mrs. Hansen stopped by. She said Alice had asked her to let you know she would be here soon. It was a pleasant visit and I enjoyed it. In all these years that we've been neighbors, she's never stopped by before."

Stephen stared at his mother then looked away quickly, hoping she did not notice the excitement he felt.

He could think of no adequate reply. After a short silence his mother continued. "I guess she came because of Alice."

When he still did not comment, she continued, "If you have time, see if you can help your father. You know how he gets. He's had that roof fixed so many times and it still leaks when the rain comes from the north."

Stephen was reluctant to explain to his mother everything between Alice and him was amorphous, undecided. Written correspondence had clarified nothing. Only physical separation intensified his feelings--life without Alice was dull and aimless. Once he feared rejection, now he faced a lifetime of loneliness. Alice's sporadic letters, at first full of excitement about her new studies, had become dispirited. For a time there were no letters, then suddenly the news that she was coming home. She had even sent her mother as a goodwill ambassador to make that announcement in person.

"I'll go down and look in on Father," he said.

His mother sighed. "I hope everything works out for you, Stephen," she said, turning back to her drawing. "Things do, sometimes. They have for me."

Driving away Stephen believed that he although he did not seem to be thinking clearly he could at least be the traditional dutiful son, obeying his mother and helping his father. Such behavior was a sign of constancy in a society where much had changed and was still changing. He noticed that rough waves had piled up hillocks of sand and seaweed along the beach during the night. Now the sea-change had taken place. The surface was calm and the motion of the waves soothingly soporific.

CHAPTER TWELVE

Stephen, an increasingly confident driver, was now capable of observing the road critically and scrutinizing the bordering fields with an acquisitive eye. He did both as he drove east toward Christiansted the following morning reflecting that the Transfer Ceremony had become more than a ritual to remember. The soil where sugar, cotton, indigo and tobacco had grown in past centuries, was about to undergo a metamorphosis into the land where prosaic dwellings for Americans would sprout. Plantations nourished by the blood of slaves would be replaced by utilitarian housing symbolic of military rule. He wondered what shapes and patterns would appear on the fields and hills of Saint Croix and where he would fit in this new world.

The rain, although heavy, was followed by a warm, steady wind from the north. The roads were dry, with no noticeable damage. The grass was turning from brown to green and dust had been washed from the gleaming leaves of the mahogany trees that shaded the road. He noticed that the ruins of Estate Hogansburg, just east of Frederiksted town, were being cleared. Acacia, which had grown into thorny trees over years of neglect, had been cut to the ground. A dirt driveway was discernible, tire tracks of an automobile clear in the soft dirt. The ruins of the great house were visible, majestic and magical. Stephen was overcome with an impulse he recognized as irrational, nevertheless filling him with joy. He wanted to restore those ruins and install Alice as the chatelaine.

While continuing his effort to locate potholes and washed-way shoulders of the road, a suppressed memory surfaced. The scene in front of him faded from his consciousness as he remembered his mother telling him that the estate had once belonged to the Atwater family, one of the many Fireburn stories recounted around the family dinner table. Hogansburg, like so many other estates destroyed in 1878 by workers seeking higher wages, had lain in ruins throughout Stephen's lifetime, the grass uncut, the only signs of life some resilient trees growing between the loosened stones of crumbling walls. The Atwater family had returned to England just after the hurricane of 1916. Rumor had it that a providential inheritance rescued them from complete ruin.

Wondering if it were possible to acquire the land, Stephen decided that perhaps his father would know what prompted the clearing. Vestrymen from St. Paul's Anglican Church in Frederiksted were in close contact with their counterparts in St. John's in Christiansted, where the Atwaters had been members. He could also check the property records in Government House, but that would be sure to cause speculation, evoke questions he was not prepared to answer.

When he arrived later than usual at Government House, the Administrator was relieved to hear that the roads were in good condition. Mrs. Warner personally invited Stephen to lunch and was in a particularly good mood. The commendation her husband had received for the successful completion of the mosquito eradication campaign, in addition to the favorable report on his other efforts to improve the conditions on the island, made her feel they had every right to request transfer home or even retirement.

"I don't wish to appear unpatriotic," she said, "but we deserve it. We've lived all these years in fever-ridden lands. I had to send my son away to school at an early age. The minute the war ends, I want to go back where I feel welcome for a change. I'm tired of being one of a small group who doesn't really belong."

"My dear, I know you're tired of living away from home, but be fair," the Administrator said. "We've had some good times. These commendations prove the Navy thinks I've done some good, thank God. Sometimes I've wondered. Stephen's family and friends have been kind and helpful and Ralph Henry hasn't been all bad, thanks to Stephen."

"Oh, I didn't mean you, Stephen," Mrs. Warner said. "You're like one of us. You remind me so much of my own son, you know that. I don't understand why you don't come back to America."

"I like it here," Stephen said, trying to speak gently. Mrs. Warner had finished her sherry quickly and he was sure it was not her first. "Have you noticed all the land clearing, sir?"

"Yes, I have. You know that Lieutenant Hokansen is retiring and planning to stay here? He has bought some land, I believe."

They managed to discuss roads, waterways and land clearing for the rest of the luncheon. Mrs. Warner, nodding, made excuses to leave the table before dessert was served. Stephen returned to his office to study some Danish maps he had requested, which recorded the boundaries of the old plantations. He decided to study them more carefully at a later date and left his office as early as he could, anxious to see if any rain damage had occurred at the Christiansted store.

When he arrived the doors were closed and there was no sign of Mark. Alarmed, he drove out to Shoys. It was not like his brother to leave his business without good reason.

Bright sunlight revealed the care with which Mark and Karen had restored the old gatehouse of Shoys Plantation. Waiting for an answer to his knock, Stephen admired the color of the frames of the windows and the solid hurricane shutters, a green so pale the wood faded into the old stone, a color and décor not seen in Frederiksted, which favored white gingerbread trimming, nor in Christiansted, where the imposing official structures stood as the Danes had built them, in their fading yellow glory.

All seemed quiet. Small puddles of water were evaporating rapidly leaving traces of their previous size in the damp earth. Stephen was tempted to call, "Inside!" in the local manner but instead knocked again, loudly, several times, before Mark came to the door. As Stephen looked at his brother's face, the words of greeting stuck in his throat.

"What's the matter, Mark?" Stephen finally said, without preliminaries.

"I'm glad you've come. You couldn't have come at a better time, as a matter of fact. Do come in. Please excuse Karen. She's very upset."

His sister-in-law was seated on the antique sofa, one hand gripping the carefully polished mahogany side. Her eyes were red and her long blonde hair was hanging in a disheveled mass on her shoulders. She made an effort to rise, but Stephen stopped her by bending over to kiss her cheek.

"I was admiring your house as I came in," he said awkwardly, unable to think of anything else to say.

Mark broke in impatiently.

"The strangest thing has happened. We wouldn't discuss this with anyone else, of course, because it concerns the family. Someone delivered a letter to the store last night, or very early this morning. I found it when I went in, pushed under the main door to the storeroom, the one I always open first. Since it was addressed to Karen, I brought it home with me at lunchtime. I wish I had opened it and destroyed it. Here. Read it."

The letter was short and clear, the words as bold as the dark, black ink, signed in large letters, "Lily". She accused Karen of deserting her dearest friend when she was in need of help. Lily, who had done everything for Karen, brought her to America, found her a husband, was now being ignored and neglected. She also accused Mark of coercing her poor, sick father into selling a large portion of his valuable land on Beeston Hill, with which Mark now intended to make a fortune. She gave them an ultimatum of two weeks to apologize for the above treatment and rescind the sale, or she would take her case to the Administrator.

Stephen looked at them both, too surprised to comment. Mark broke the silence.

"It's all untrue, of course. Damned lies. Karen's been busy fixing up the house and had little time for anything else. Then when she thought she might be pregnant, Dr. Hokansen suggested rest and quiet. We invited Lily to come here several times. She would ask if you were coming, and if you weren't, she would make some excuse to stay away, say she couldn't leave her father and he was too ill to come. Now she implies I secretly made contact with him to cheat him out of his land. I've never even talked with the man."

"She has no legal case," Stephen said, feeling inadequate as he said it.

"She's crazy, she must be," Karen said between sobs. "I've always loved Lily. How could she say such things about me, about us, if she weren't crazy?"

Looking at the pale and shivering Karen, Stephen became concerned. He glanced at Mark, who responded by sitting on the sofa beside his wife and taking her in his arms. As Mark assured Karen that her health was the only important thing and his brother would straighten things out, Stephen walked over to the window and looked westward in the direction of Buelow's Minde. The thick walls surrounding the window were wide enough for him to sit on as he tried to think of what to do. His first impulse was to offer to go see Lily, but reasoned that if she had turned against Mark and Karen, she would certainly be hostile to him.

Mark's worry was his wife. "I wish Mother felt well enough to come stay with Karen for a few days. She has no family here and Lily was her closest friend."

"I don't think that's a good idea," Stephen said quickly. "I'll ask Dr. Hokansen to stop by. He's been coming to Christiansted frequently now that he has a car."

Stephen bade farewell to the two forlorn figures on the sofa. As he got into the car, he noticed that the sky over the western end of the island had darkened, blotting out the sunset. Before he was out of the driveway raindrops splattered the windshield and by the time he reached the main road driving was difficult. Forced to go very slowly, he felt a sudden longing for an intelligent and experienced horse that could follow the road and allow him to concentrate on Lily's strange behavior. He remembered the very different days when he had ridden home toward a welcoming sunset, certain of warm greeting from his mother and a smile from Alice.

Stephen decided to stop at the hospital to see if Dr. Hokansen was available and to inform him of Mark's request. Miranda Muckle was standing on the steps talking to a young woman. Even though he only saw her back, Stephen was certain it was not a mirage. It *was* Alice. Miranda stopped talking when she saw Stephen. He was running toward them by the time Alice turned to greet him. With Miranda watching closely Stephen settled for an avuncular hug.

"How wonderful to see you! I didn't know you were here."

"I just got in last night. We, the research group, we've been in St. John for a week. After a site for the laboratories was selected and I introduced them to a few people, they told me to come home to St. Croix until they got the lab set up. So here I am. I was hoping you might stop by. I could use a ride home. We'll talk tomorrow, Miss Muckle, if that's all right?"

Miranda nodded. A worried frown creased her forehead but Stephen didn't care. He was anxious to get Alice out of sight, which was not easy. Miranda promised to deliver Stephen's message to Dr. Hokansen to visit Marks' wife but remained on the steps of the hospital watching them drive north down Strand Street toward Mahogany Road.

Before turning into the Hansen driveway, Stephen stopped by the side of the road in the shade of a giant mahogany.

Alice leaned back in the seat. "It's so nice and cool here. I'd forgotten about the sea breezes."

"I thought you'd forgotten about *me*."

"Of course I didn't. I thought at least you would kiss me hello."

"Not with Miranda Muckle watching."

"She's not watching now."

"No. We must talk first. These months of waiting, not knowing...I really must know how you feel about me, whether you would consider marrying me, and how you feel about, well, life, everything, I guess."

When Alice smiled, Stephen realized how much she had changed. The youthful intensity had been replaced by a steady, thoughtful gaze. The rounded velvety cheeks were hollower, paler. She seemed tired, yet at the same time strong and sure of herself. Her smile was sad.

"Well, Stephen, you seem to know what you want. I never felt that about you before. I was in love with you, but you never said anything. And as for how I feel about you now, well, over these months I've felt a lot of different ways about a lot of people, but mostly I thought about you. It would take a long time to tell you all about it. It was hopeless to try to explain in letters, because by the time I wrote the letter, I would feel differently. Sometimes I even thought I wouldn't come home, you know."

"No. I didn't know. Tell me, I'll listen."

He listened a long time. The sun was setting before Alice finished her halting recitation of exciting studies that were suddenly replaced by desperate demands for the active help of trainees. Studies were abandoned so the student nurses could assist the regular nurses in dealing with an epidemic. All of the hospital beds were full, including cots in the hall, with victims of influenza. Knowing that they themselves could be infected at any moment, the young women worked long hours with little respite.

The outings she had initially enjoyed with her brother and sister-in-law at the jazz clubs of Harlem ceased when public places were closed because of public health precautions. Worse still, even before the epidemic, her brother had told her not to go outside of Harlem. When she ignored his warnings, she could not comprehend nor accept the way she had been treated in the department stores and ignored in the streets.

"It was true you know, what that man said in his book. I was an invisible woman. As far as white people were concerned, I didn't exist. I decided to go to meetings of the Urban League with my brother and sister-in-law".

She soon shared their sense of outrage against the world outside, Alice said.

"I hated you for a while," Alice said, "really hated you. I hated a lot of people, but mostly you." Stephen was relieved to see her smile.

"Then those stories came out in the newspapers," Alice continued. "About how awful life was in the Virgin Islands, how the workers were oppressed and people lived in huts, and ate weird food. They didn't believe me, my brother's friends, when I told them my family owned had a nice house and a lot of property and I could go anywhere I wanted without being afraid and everyone treated me and my family decently. They thought Antilleans, or West Indians, or whatever kind of savages we were, lived in the bush. I told them we lived better than most people in Harlem and we got along with white people quite well most of the time and many of us were of mixed blood anyway. They hated it at the meetings when I spoke up about our life here. My brother Richard knew the truth, but he said talking about it didn't help The Cause. He wanted people to be angry and protest. I got so mad at him. And then at the hospital, with all those young people dying, and it began to seem like so much nonsense, all that fighting about nothing. I couldn't think clearly about much, but that was clear."

It was getting dark. Alice's voice was faltering and she was clearly becoming agitated. Stephen did not want to take her home in such a condition.

"We can talk about this more tomorrow," he said. "Let's go see my mother. She stops painting as soon as the light fades. This would be a good time. She'll give you some lemongrass tea. Calms you down and makes the world look better. That's what you always said when you prepared it for her."

"All right," Alice said. "But let me tell you this first. Something really good happened. These doctors came in to the hospital, white doctors, from a place called Rockefeller University, looking for me. They were planning to set up a research station in the Virgin Islands. They had chosen a place where no cases of influenza had been reported. And one of their colleagues, a doctor at Harlem hospital, told them about me, a native Virgin Islander, a nurse who had almost finished her training. They offered me a job. They wanted me to come back here with them, help them get settled in St. John, and work in the lab. At a really good salary. They didn't even think about what color I was, just that they needed me to help in the work they wanted to do, to find a way to stop the dying. They needed *me*. Said I could help them. *Me*. Help *them*. I hadn't even finished all my training yet and they were all experienced doctors. Instead of being invisible, I was important."

"Always. You always were. Important," Stephen said, turning on the motor and maneuvering on to the road.

"But the best thing," she continued, "the finny thing, was that after I talked to those nice doctors who were so polite and offered me the chance to do research, something I'd always wanted, all of a sudden, just like that, I stopped being confused. I didn't hate anyone any more. And I fell in love with you all over again, Stephen. I realized how much you were like them. Respectful, polite, offering me a chance at a good life. I wanted to be with you and hoped you wanted me. That's when I wrote Mommy, asking her to call on your mother. I had to be sure she would be welcome, we were equals, neighbors. And she was, welcome, I mean. Said your mother spent most of the afternoon talking about music, how fortunate people are who have musically talented offspring."

Stephen laughed. "That sounds like mother."

"Don't laugh. I'm serious. Do you understand what I'm talking about? How I feel about my job, my work? My life was spared when so many died, are dying."

"I understand," Stephen said. "I went to law school to please my father, but I was a lawyer before I ever went to school. On a small island either you obey the law and get along or you sink into chaos. I knew that early on, I don't know how. Something in the air, maybe. I don't know. But it's why I want to live here."

For the first time Alice smiled cheerfully. "Not the air, you idiot. It's your parents, don't you realize that? Your father, he talks funny sometimes, but he's a real Christian, Daddy says. And your mother, well, she lives in a world of her own, a better world maybe. You're right, let's go see her. I want to see how she is."

"Then we had better hurry," Stephen said. "It's getting dark and Dr. Hokansen insists she eat at regular hours and retire early. Thank God she does what the doctor tells her to for a change."

CHAPTER THIRTEEN

In contrast to his inner turmoil, the world around Stephen seemed routinely peaceful. Sunday began in the usual quiet fashion. Kristin Markham, feeling well, asked Stephen to accompany her to the Lutheran Church. His father, as usual, had left earlier to be sure the Anglican Church was in proper order for the two Sunday masses. As a child, Stephen had once asked why his parents did not attend the same church. The answer permitted no argument. Cedric Markham was already established as an Anglican vestryman at the time of their marriage, and Kristin's grandfather was a Lutheran clergyman. As he grew older Stephen realized this was more a statement of autonomy on his mother's part than religious conviction. The Danes, and those with some Danish ancestry, attended the Lutheran church and enjoyed meeting their friends and conversing in Danish.

But this Sunday after the services, as parishioners chatted in the churchyard, Kristin Markham made an uncharacteristic and seemingly spontaneous gesture. Stephen dutifully accompanied his mother as she joined the Hansens. Kristin Markham congratulated Mrs. Hansen on the choice of hymns.

"It's so important, I think, to find hymns suitable for the church season. You play Bach so well. Only music like that can make me feel that the pentacostal spirit of hope and renewal is with us."

As Mrs. Hansen smiled her acknowledgement of the compliment, Kristin invited the Hansens to La Grange for "a simple family luncheon". Stephen hoped he concealed his surprise. Alice seemed to take the invitation as a matter of course. After a moment's hesitation and exchange of glances, the Hansens accepted.

As soon as Stephen and his mother arrived home, he realized that her spontaneity was a deception. Salt fish gundy and chilled maabi, local dishes that demanded careful preparation, were already placed on a wooden picnic table in the front courtyard ready to be served. Kristin Markham went to the kitchen to confer with the cook, who ordinarily did not work on Sundays. She rejoined Stephen in time to greet the Hansens as they arrived.

Alice, with easy familiarity, preceded her parents to the shaded table Kristen Markham indicated. The Hansens, waiting until asked to do so, sat down choosing chairs on either side of their daughter. Their stiff backs did not relax in the cushioned comfort.

Mr. Hansen was a stocky man, light skinned with a bristling black mustache. His posture reminded Stephen of the military guards at Government House and he remembered that Alice's paternal grandfather had been an officer in the Danish militia. Mr. Hansen sat in his chair as if guarding his daughter. His wife was more relaxed, with dark velvety skin, sharp features and large, dark eyes, her hair pulled back tightly in a straightening bun. The overall impression was one of neatness and clothes carefully chosen.

They were barely seated when Cedric Markham arrived. He greeted the guests formally but cordially and remarked on the heat. He then asked Stephen to serve the maabi.

Stephen remembered how often and with what grace, Alice had served him cold drinks while she was caring for his mother. He was grateful to reach the lesser level of competence, to be able to fill he glasses without mishap.

The amenities began with guesses about the age of the giant flamboyant tree the branches of which shaded the entire table. It was reputed to be one of the oldest and largest on the island.

Stephen was amused that the conversation which ensued was so familiar, following the same predictable pattern of comments heard in the domain of the planters. Observations on the recent rain, reports of how much had fallen on what parts of the island and predictions of what might occur now that hurricane season was upon them

Despite the frivolous chatter, Stephen was sure the purpose of the gathering was serious and clear to all. This was a formal recognition by his parents of the intentions of their offspring, planned by his mother, acquiesced to by his father and hopefully acceptable to the Hansens.

Kristin Markham was clearly contented, listening with a smile as her husband discussed with Mrs. Hansen the relative merits of Anglican and Lutheran hymns. Stephen made an effort to sound knowledgeable as he described to Mr. Hansen the problems of importing automobiles. Alice appeared to be listening to both conversations, alternating her attention.

At one moment Cedric Markham broke off his discussion to ask his wife if Mark and Karen were coming, adding that he hadn't seen them at church.

"Stephen said Karen wasn't feeling well when he saw them the other evening. Perhaps we can all get together before Alice leaves. I hope you like St. John, Alice. Stephen told me he might consider setting up his law practice there."

"Oh, I hope not," Alice said. "I've promised my parents that when the two years of my contract are up, I will move back to St. Croix."

Mrs. Hansen looked alarmed for a moment, then laughed nervously. "Indeed she did promise. My son Richard says he doesn't plan to return to Saint Croix and I don't want to lose Alice too."

Mr. Hansen reinforced her statement. "I understand why some young people leave the island when they have no employment or a means of livelihood here. But Alice will have work at the hospital and if Richard does not return, she will inherit our estate."

Stephen was beginning to feel as if he were present at some medieval disposition of assets at the time of betrothal and longed to get way, to be alone with Alice. Instead, he tried to think of something more, anything of interest, about automobiles.

To Stephen's relief, Mr. Hansen spoke. "I've heard rumors at the rum factory that as soon as the war is over the American Congress will pass a law making the sale of alcoholic beverages illegal. Have you heard anything about that, Stephen? Or perhaps you have, Mr. Markham? I understand many of the churches are backing the so-called Prohibition Movement."

"Not the Anglican, or Episcopal, Church as they call it in America." Cedric Markham said. "I must confess I haven't paid much attention to it. All of our prayers have been for a quick end to the war, which, thank God, seems to be in sight."

At this point Kristin Markham, noticeably pale, begged to be excused pleading fatigue. The Hansens, murmuring "Thank you" prepared to leave. Stephen, unable to speak to Alice privately, announced in front of everyone that he would try to get back to Frederiksted early on Monday afternoon to spend time with her.

"Meet me at the hospital," she said. "I promised Miss Muckle I would drop by."

Now that he was alone with his father, Stephen asked, "Why are you looking concerned? Is something the matter? You don't object to my marrying Alice, do you? I didn't have a chance to discuss it with you before Mother...."

"Don't worry," his father said. "Your mother has made things quite clear. She mentioned how appropriate it was that you had received your epiphany in the season of Pentecost and had decided to stop being as indecisive as Hamlet. How can one argue with a statement like that? Never underestimate your mother's ability to achieve what she wants. In any case, you're an adult, Stephen, and you've shown great understanding of my hopes and fears for the church. If the church endures, our society cannot fail. I've always believed that only God should judge the actions of men. No. My worries are much more mundane. I set Mark up in business in Christiansted when he married. I was just wondering what I should do for you."

Stephen said that the expensive education he had received was more than enough, but his father persisted. Finally, Stephen mentioned the Hogansberg property.

Mr. Markham nodded. "I'll look into it. In the meantime, you might ask your cousin Douglas what he knows about this new law."

Stephen did not have to seek out his cousin. He was waiting in Stephen's office the following morning.

"I suppose you saw the article Ralph Henry wrote," Douglas said, omitting the customary "Good Morning".

"No. I haven't."

"Well for once I agree with him. The Americans have gone too far. They are going to ruin us. We'll starve to death. Don't they realize that the sale of rum is our main source of income? You're a lawyer. Do something about this Prohibition thing."

"First of all, I don't see what I can do. If I remember my classes in constitutional law correctly, there has to be an Amendment."

"That's what they plan to do. Amend the Constitution. A group of fanatical women taking advantage of the fact that all the real men are off fighting a war."

"Don't you want to sit down, Douglas? I'll discuss this with the Administrator as soon as possible."

"No. I don't want to sit down. The Americans! With all their talk of saving the world for democracy, have they ever asked us how we wanted to be governed? Coming in here and criticizing the way we live, as if it's some sort of crime to play polo and tennis and have civilized parties. We're Europeans, our traditions are anyway. We were better off under the Danes. What have the Americans done for us except kill a few mosquitoes?"

"Is that what Ralph Henry said?"

"No. You know it isn't. He's learned how to manipulate the Americans and you've helped him. You've betrayed us.

Our families were here long before most of these workers. We can see right through Ralph Henry and his labor movement, even if the Americans can't. For God's sake, Stephen, it's not a group of ignorant natives whose livelihoods are being threatened, it's us, the people who count on this island. If we can't sell our rum we'll go bankrupt, lose power. The old order will break down and nobody will know what's what or who's who."

"I don't see what I can do," Stephen said truthfully.

"That's the whole point. *We* can't do anything. We're powerless with no rights at all. Admit the truth. The Americans are going to destroy us and we can't do a thing about it." Douglas strode out, colliding with the Administrator at the doorway.

"Pardon me," Douglas said. "Good morning to you, sir." He glared at the Administrator for a moment before he hurried away.

"What's bothering your cousin?" Captain Warner asked as he sat down on the chair reserved for visitors. Stephen, usually summoned to the Administrator's office, found this reversal of positions disconcerting, as if their relative roles had changed. For a moment, he empathized with Douglas about a change in order. It did disturb one's thinking.

"He's heard reports that the sale of alcoholic beverages is about to become illegal in the United States and assumes it would apply to the territories as well."

"I'm afraid it's true. I've become so involved with problems here I haven't paid that much attention to what's going on at home. But all that's about to change. I've asked to be relieved immediately. My wife and I will leave on the first transport available. The Governor will be sending someone over from St. Thomas to replace me and the new Administrator will be bringing his own staff. I know you've been wanting to set up your own law practice, so I hope this sudden change won't be a disappointment to you."

"But why, sir? Why are you leaving now?"

"We've received word that our son is very ill with influenza and if my wife had wings she'd be there already. I can't deny her the right to go to our son as soon as possible and she needs me with her. She's been through too much with me and I've done all I can do here. Ironic, isn't it? I'm sent here to eradicate tropical fevers and my son falls ill of some dreaded plague back home in America."

Protests formed in Stephen's mind, but he uttered none of them, unsure of what he really wanted to say.

"I'll miss you, sir," he finally said.

"Thank you. We'll talk again before I leave. Would you please tell your father I would appreciate a visit from him?"

Stephen nodded. The Administrator walked over to the window that offered a view of Christiansted town.

"I've liked this island. I hope we did some good here. The Navy, I mean. After a while you begin to wonder. And once you begin to have doubts about whether you're right about things, you lose your sense of discipline and you're not very effective as an Administrator. Well, carry on, Stephen."

Stephen sought out his brother when he left his office. He was relieved to find him at the store, locking up for the day.

"Karen's feeling better, I assume, or you wouldn't be here?" he said.

"Yes, thank God. She's quite all right again. Lily came by and apologized. Admitted she gets agitated sometimes from that medicine she's taking."

"What medicine?"

"Something to get thin. She gets if from a doctor in Puerto Rico. You know how much weight she's lost. It does make her very nervous, Karen says. Lily's not supposed to drink when she takes it, but she does. Anyway, Lily has said she's sorry and Karen wants to forget the whole thing. She and Lily have been so close. Karen needs companionship so much just now. I wish Mother…"

"Has Lily seen a doctor here? About the medication?"

"No, she doesn't want to. She says the doctors here haven't prescribed anything to help her father. I went to see old man Loring, by the way. He told me he had suggested to Lily that I be consulted about selling their property and she was furious. She accused him of ruining her chances of making a decent marriage if she doesn't have an estate and a good income from the cattle."

"So everything's all right now?"

When Mark agreed that it seemed that way for the moment, at least, Stephen informed him of the Administrator's decision to leave as soon as possible.

"Then you won't be coming to Christiansted any more, if you're going to start a practice in Frederiksted?"

"Not on a daily basis."

"Well, I hope you'll come up for dinner with us, now that Karen's feeling better. I know you enjoy her cooking."

"Of course, if you'll include Alice. We're about to announce our engagement."

Mark stared at him. Stephen waited.

Finally, Mark said, "You'll probably be asked to resign from the Country Club."

Stephen laughed, but regretted it when he saw his brother flush.

"I know," Mark said. "You don't care, do you? It doesn't matter that you're embarrassing the family. Now Karen will be really upset. How am I going to tell her?"

"I don't know, Mark," Stephen said. "And you're right. I don't care. No one's embarrassed except you and your ... wife."

Stephen left quickly. He had almost called Karen "stupid", had almost told his brother that his mother far preferred Alice to Karen as a daughter-in-law. A herd of goats, in the middle of the dirt road leading out of Estate Shoys, blocked his path. He focused his anger on them, blowing the car horn in frustration. The goats merely looked at him with amused, wicked eyes and moved their upright short tails back and forth. Their unconcern increased his frustration but all he could do was wait as the thin animals munched on the patches of new, green grass.

CHAPTER FOURTEEN

Stephen accepted his father's offer to convert part of the warehouse into two rooms for a lawyer's office. He needed income to get married.

Alice had informed him that she intended to spend her last few days in Saint Croix helping Miranda Muckle at the hospital.

"I'll spend every moment of every evening with you, Stephen, I promise, but I must do something worth while during the day. I'm a nurse and people are dying in an epidemic. I can't enjoy myself swimming and sailing. Just can't. I want to work."

Stephen was grateful for this decision, as it freed him to do the same. He was surprised by how much he missed the routine of going to Christiansted every day, greeting the guard at the entrance to Government House and sitting down at a desk almost completely covered with neat piles of paper.

He did his best to replicate the office he had left. He had one of his father's workmen paint the walls the same dim yellow of official buildings. He re-arranged the law books he had hardly looked at for months, and had a sign made announcing he was an Attorney-at-Law.

Almost immediately, he had a client. Beulah Pemberton walked in the door before the paint was dry. When she came in he was disappointed, as he had hoped his first client would be someone who would pay well. Then Beulah surprised him. She announced she was tired of paying rent to "dat tief", wanted to buy some property and had the money to do so. She needed a good lawyer because the owner was not eager to sell.

"I want dat building across the street. Yes, dat big one. I can live upstairs and have me shop below, de way you merchants do. Dat old house, it's plenty big. It's all boarded up since dose two old maids died and left it to their nephew. He lives in New York. Don' wan' it, but don' wan' nobody else to have it."

"What's his name?"

"Caspar Holstein. He's a friend of Ralph Henry's. You know Ralph and I don' see eye to eye. I know he a lawyer, but he don' lawyer none. Jus' for hisself, his paper and his union. Only help others when he gets a piece of dere property. *You* got to get dat one passel fo' me. *You* go speak to Ralph."

Stephen promised to do what he could. As he opened the door for Beulah to leave, he saw Lily sitting in her parked car across the street. She waved, smiled, got out of the car and walked purposefully toward his office ignoring Beulah as they passed each other.

"What a pretty little sign, Stephen. So you've finally made the move. I just had to see it. I've just made my first drive to Frederiksted, all by myself. I wanted to see how you were doing."

Stephen invited her to come in, warning her that the paint might still be wet in places.

Lily, looking around curiously, sat down on a dusty chair. "Was that the cleaning woman who just went out? She didn't do a very good job."

"She's a client," Stephen said, determined not to get annoyed. "She owns a bake shop. I've known her since I was a little boy."

"You always were sentimental, but I hope you're not a complete fool. You're not really going to *marry* a native girl, are you?"

"If you're referring to Alice Hansen, yes, I am."

Lily sat up tensely in her chair, a snake ready to strike. "How can you be such an idiot? You and I could make such a good marriage. I'm a wealthy woman with a large estate. You and I have been close since we were children. Our mothers were friends. Those are the kinds of things that make good marriages and keep families like ours in control here. I need someone who can help me manage my property."

"I thought you had employed Ramón for that. And besides, I'm in love with Alice Hansen. I'm sorry if I ever gave you the impression that I wasn't serious about her."

"I'm not a fool like you, Stephen. Ramón works for me, takes orders from me, he knows his place. I want an educated, well-born husband, an elegant home, children born of good families. It's not fair that that silly goose Karen should have all this and I just have to stand by and watch. There is a bond between us, Stephen, you can't deny that. We can at least discuss this like two old friends. Let's get out of this damp little hole and go for a ride in my car."

"No. Thank you. I meet Alice every afternoon at the hospital at five, and it's almost five now."

"Really? You meet her there every afternoon? How devoted of you! How like a sheep dog! I warn you, these native women age rapidly. She won't look like much in a few years. You'll be wanting to get rid of her."

Stephen was tempted to throw Lily bodily out of the office but restrained himself by gripping the desk.

"You'd better leave, Lily."

"I'm going. Just remember what I said. If you don't, you'll be sorry."

He watched as she drove away, too fast, scattering chickens. He was grateful that there were no pedestrians in her way.

Alice was waiting for him on the front steps of the hospital. She looked weary but content.

"It's official, Stephen. I'll be leaving for St. John in the middle of next week. Finally, the buildings are ready for occupancy and we must get started on our project. There's still talk of submarines so the ship will be going to St. Thomas first, then I'll take a small boat to St. John. Why don't you come with me for a few days?"

He was tempted. "I'd like to, but I can't. I have a client. I just can't walk out on her. When will you be coming back?"

"You read my contract. We get a week off every four weeks since we work such long hours and they want us to stay healthy. You said you have a client? That's wonderful. Who is it?"

Alice knew Beulah well and urged Stephen to do his best for her. He in turn said that as soon as he had completed a few cases successfully, he would visit St. John. He added he needed Ralph Henry's help in expediting Beulah's request.

Ralph Henry was reluctant when approached. He considered Beulah "uppity" and a "badmouth" and feared she would become even more so as a property owner.

A little flattery helped. Stephen reminded the newspaper editor that he, as President of the Workers' Union, was now a large landholder himself and the owner of an automobile as well. In a position of such responsibility, one had an obligation to help an enterprising business woman. Ralph Henry finally agreed to cable Caspar Holstein, whose frequent donations to the Labor Union proved he was doing too well in New York City to ever return to the Virgin Islands.

"He has sworn he will never sell to the "oppressors", but he might consider selling to a native," Ralph Henry said. "He's had some bad experiences trying to buy property in New York City. If the white people up there won't sell to him, why should he sell to them? But maybe he'll consider Beulah."

"I would appreciate your help."

"Don't go yet. I want a favor in return. I want to buy land in the middle of the island, near the cane fields, so the workers can each buy a plot and build themselves a little house."

"I heard something about that. That's quite a project. You're thinking of several hundred workers."

"But it can be done?"

"Maybe. Let me look up some of the deeds, talk to some of the owners, see what can be worked out." Remembering his own longing to own Estate Hogansberg, Stephen empathized with the workers' desire for a piece of land.

"You're not looking too well these days," Ralph Henry said. "Is everything all right?"

"I'm sorry to see the Administrator leave in such unhappy circumstances. He's a troubled, not sure if he governed properly. Not even sure if the Navy should be governing at all. To be honest, I'm not sure myself."

"You know what's wrong with you, don't you? I've always known and I'm going to tell you. You're a black man walking around in a white skin."

Stephen tried to smile. "Maybe you're right," he said.

Ralph Henry followed him to the door, warning him about Lily's driving.

"I saw her when she drove into town the other morning. All over the road, and going fast. Please tell the Administrator that people should be tested before they are allowed to drive. Women have no business running machines anyway."

"I don't know whether I'll see Captain Warner before he leaves. Write an editorial. I'm sure the Navy doesn't want wild drivers on the road."

Cedric Markham informed his wife and son at dinner that evening that the Administrator had secured passage for himself and his wife the following week. They would be going as far as St. Thomas on the same transport as Alice. Navy ships would be coming in less frequently now that the Allies were obviously winning the war and the Panama Canal was no longer threatened.

"I spent some time with Captain Warner this morning. His son is seriously ill, a fact he is concealing from his wife. He wants me to arrange to have some special prayers said in church for his son's recovery. I will speak to Father Morrow."

"Say some prayers for Alice, too," Kristin Markham said. "Going off to work in a laboratory full of deadly germs."

Cedric Markham nodded. "I'm thinking of inviting a few people to say good-bye to the Administrator. Just a small group. We can meet in the reception room of my office. The Administrator wants no fuss at all, says to save that for the new staff coming in. But we can't let him go without some sort of farewell. A man who has spent his career wiping out fever in the American tropics, and now his son falls ill from a worse plague at home. He deserves our prayers. The ship will be sailing about six in the evening on Wednesday, the last I heard. Could you ask Beulah to arrange something in the way of refreshments, Stephen? And let your brother and his wife know?"

Stephen nodded his agreement. Saddened by the latest news about the Warners's son, he was even more depressed by the realization that yet another good-bye to Alice was just days away.

"When are you getting married, Stephen?" his mother asked as if reading his thoughts.

"I don't know," Stephen said, startled by her abruptness.

"Well, perhaps you should set a date before Alice leaves."

"I was waiting until I was getting some clients, making some money."

"Oh, for heaven's sake," his mother said. "You're not penniless. You and Alice can live here until you get your own home. I admit it will be a little odd, going back and forth to St. John, but it is wartime and Alice is an unusual young woman. A lawyer is freer than most to travel. Get some clients in St. John."

Stephen glanced at his father, who merely nodded, as if his mind were elsewhere.

"You will get in touch with Mark? I stopped by the store to see him when I was in Christiansted, but he wasn't there. Everything looked in order though. It was a good idea to open up in Christiansted."

As promised, Stephen relayed his father's invitation to Mark the following morning. His brother was busy putting up cans of paint on the display shelves and did not interrupt his work to converse with Stephen.

"We'll be there," he said coldly. "And tell mother Karen and I would like to stop by and see her afterwards. I don't suppose she'll be going in to town?"

"No. She's not going." Stephen did not mention that his mother planned her own goodbye dinner for Alice the evening before the sailing.

He was unable to see the Administrator who was busy meeting with his staff. Not wishing to intrude on these final farewells, Stephen drove back to Frederiksted reflecting that the hurricane season was just about over. The roads had held up, the fields were green, the dam was full and November, just a few days away, was traditionally a rainy month.

He went to Beulah's bake shop and arranged for the food. It was hard to convince her that the preparations had to be simple, cold foods, as meals would be available on the ship.

"See if you can get some ice. Send your grandson up to Christiansted to the ice-house by the wharf. The ship sails at six, Father says. Captain Warner and his wife will arrive around four. It's still pretty warm at sunset on the waterfront."

Stephen remembered the first time he had met the Administrator at the reception after the Transfer ceremony and how he had kept wiping the perspiration from his face. Ice would be welcome, Stephen was sure.

Alice had informed him that she planned to leave her luggage on the ship and say good-bye to her parents there. She would join him at the offices of Markham and Sons after her final farewell to Miranda Muckle at the hospital.

The guests looked as funereal as he felt, Stephen thought, as he seated them in the reception room of his father's office.

Captain Warner, who arrived alone, was grateful for the iced drink Stephen served him as soon as he entered. The Administrator had lost weight, Stephen noted, and with it the air of self-confidence associated with authority.

"My wife isn't feeling too well and is resting on the ship. She sends a special good-bye to you, Stephen, and says she will write you a note." He turned to greet the Anglican rector. "Good afternoon, Father Morrow. I would like to thank you for your prayers."

"You're quite welcome, Captain," Father Morrow said. "I'm sorry to see you leave. You've made a lot of improvements here."

"Indeed you have," Beulah said loudly from beside a large desk, cleared of papers and laden with Danish cheeses and crackers. "The Navy's done good by Beulah, dat's for true."

Stephen was glad to see the Administrator smile. Beulah was dressed in a bright purple silk dress, which proclaimed her a guest as well as a caterer. On another occasion, he might have felt embarrassed by her intrusive remarks but at this particular time Stephen welcomed her stout presence, radiating energy around a room full of despondence.

The arrival of Mark and Karen added tension. Karen looked around quickly, gave a small sigh, shook hands with Captain Warner and immediately sat down. Mark served his wife a drink and stood conversing with the Administrator as Ralph Henry appeared.

"It's nice of you to stop by, Mr. Henry. You are probably not sorry to see me leave," Captain Warner said.

"On the contrary, Captain," Ralph Henry said. "We'll probably get someone far worse. You did some good things, I'll grant you that. I thank you on behalf of my people."

"Well, I wish *your* people well. I prefer to think of them as *our* people. The war will soon be over and many changes will take place, I'm sure. For the better. We want only the best for the future of the Virgin Islands."

"Let's see what the people want."

Stephen, wondering where this conversation might lead, glanced at his father's face. He had never seen his father look so horrified and turned quickly to see what had appalled him. Alice was standing in the doorway, the entire front of her light dress stained with blood.

"Stephen," she said. "Come quickly. It's your cousin Lily. She's been in an accident. She's at the hospital."

Before Stephen could respond, he heard a low moan and saw Karen sag in her chair, then slump to the floor. Mark rushed to his wife's side. Without a word, Stephen followed Alice, running, down to the hospital.

CHAPTER FIFTEEN

Miranda Muckle, sitting regally in her white uniform behind a neat desk, looked very calm. One of luminous paintings from Dr. Hokansen's collection hung on the wall of the immaculate room furnished with three straight-backed chairs. The painting created an ambience so powerful Stephen had difficulty in remembering he was in a hospital. Miranda's face, in the foreground, was a congruent part of the exotic setting. Her dark skin was enhanced by the luxuriant colors, the deep greens of the leaves, the purple of the flowers. A bird with reddish beady eyes, which Stephen recognized but could not name, perched on one of the branches, its feathers the same white in which Miranda was clothed. The sterile uniform reminded Stephen that the exotic woman before him was a trained nurse, officious, meticulous in her attention to duty. Her dark eyes regarded him steadily as he made the effort to recall where he was and why he was there.

At the breakfast table Mr. Markham had informed his wife and son that he had received word that Lily was in no serious danger.

"Elias came early and left a message with Gustav that Lily was recovering. I did not speak to him personally," Cedric Markham said. "Stephen, I would appreciate it if you would visit Lily on behalf of the family."

"Of course, Father," Stephen answered. "Did Elias say anything about the accident?"

"I did not choose to speak with him, just told Gustav to send him away. I have never considered Elias a reliable person and I am too busy to spend time with such people. I have an important meeting with some of the Granard cousins this morning and it takes *them* a long time to come to the point. So I hope you will represent the family and express our concern for Lily's well-being."

A pallid Kristin Markham, whose improvement had been noticeable in recent weeks, had relapsed to languor this morning. Her hair, usually coiled like a gleaming crown around her head, was hanging in a braid down her back, seemingly dragging her energy with it.

"Lily was a very reckless driver. I heard that from everyone. I'm sure she brought this damage on herself," she said.

"Let me remind you once more, my dear, that it is not wise to believe servants' gossip," Cedric said.

"Why not? They know more about what's going on than anyone else and you'll never know the truth from Lily. Don't believe a word she tells you, Stephen."

Sitting now in Nurse Muckle's office, he waited impatiently for permission to visit Lily and wondered why it was necessary. He reminded himself to be polite and made an effort to emulate Miranda's calm. He tried to find some answers by contemplating that serene face.

"You are looking well," he said, wondering how people who dealt with life-threatening accidents and disease on a daily basis could look so imperturbable. "The nurse in the front hall said I should speak to you. When will I be able to see Lily?"

"I don't know...tomorrow...perhaps. She has two black eyes and a bandage on her neck. She says she looks too awful for anyone to see her." Miranda looked doubtful. "Lily did see that nice young Puerto Rican man who works for her-- he's a cousin of one of our trainees who says he comes from a horse-raising family in Puerto Rico. She told him she intended to go home tomorrow, no matter what, and ordered him to come fetch her. I told your father this when he came by after receiving a message I sent him. But you might try a visit later this afternoon..."

"All right," Stephen said, wondering why his father, who often complained about wasted time and effort, had insisted that Stephen come to the hospital if Lily was refusing to see visitors. "I'll try again this afternoon, in case she changes her mind." He rose to leave.

"Wait a minute. Come back. Let me tell you about the accident." Stephen could see that Miranda was hesitant to talk and choosing her words carefully. "I think you should know what happened. Lily was trying to run down Alice with her car. I know, it's shocking, and rather hard to believe, but you *should* know. Elias told me Lily's car was parked down the block all that afternoon. About five o'clock he was by the stairs sweeping with that big heavy broom he uses for out- side walks and very curious about the car, so kept watching it. Then as I stood there, saying good-bye to Lily--she was standing at the bottom of the stairs looking up at me, both Elias and I saw the car start up and head right for Alice. He threw the broom at the car, a reflex, I guess. The handle hit the glass in the front-- the windshield-- I think it's called. The car swerved enough so that the car hit the wall instead of Alice. Are you all right, Stephen? You're very pale."

"I'm all right," Stephen said. "Alice never mentioned anything like that. Are you sure, Miranda? You know how unreliable Elias is."

"It's probable Alice didn't see the car coming. She was looking up the stairs, talking to me, upset about leaving, promising to come back. I suppose I could be wrong, but I don't think so. Elias swears that's what he saw and I think he's too frightened to lie. What I don't understand is how Lily knew Alice would be there at the hospital at that time. She was obviously waiting for her."

"I told her," Stephen said. "I told her. I said I met Alice there every day at that time. Lily probably didn't know Alice was stopping by on her way to the ship, thought it was it was a regular day, just like any other."

Miranda sighed. "Well, you know Elias. The story is all over Frederiksted by now, with him the big hero. We can only hope people think he is exaggerating."

Stephen felt numb. He stared at Miranda for a few minutes. If anyone else had told him that Lily had deliberately attempted to harm Alice, he would not have believed it. However, he knew Miranda and he did believe it.

"What should I do?" Stephen finally said, helplessly.

"I don't know. When you do see Lily, I would try to impress upon her that Alice saved her life. She did, you know. The break in her leg was painful but not too serious. Dr. Hokansen set it right away and it should heal nicely. It was that partially severed artery in her neck caused by th broken glass hat could have killed her if Alice hadn't applied pressure immediately and stopped the bleeding. She's a well-trained nurse and a quick-thinking one. I'm proud of her. How much you should tell Alice about what Lily tried to do, well, I don't know. You look very pale, Stephen. Take a deep breath."

Stephen regarded Miranda mutely for a few minutes, unable to comment. He did not resist when she came over to take his pulse and sipped the water she offered him. The concern in her eyes threatened his composure. Nodding farewell, he left abruptly.

His legs grew steadier as he walked slowly along the waterfront toward *Markham and Sons*, wondering what he should do next. He recalled vividly that despite the drama of the accident and the rush to the hospital, Alice was relaxed by the time he drove her home to change her clothes and then to the ship. She was gratified that she had been able to perform successfully as a nurse and good had come of it.

Stephen, on the contrary, was sufficiently disconcerted to forget about financial responsibility and careful planning. He had impulsively asked Alice when they would be married.

"Oh, Christmas, don't you think?" Alice said without hesitation. "I get more time off then, and they may extend that a little if I say I'm getting married. Your mother and Mommy have been planning it all. November is just beginning. If we wait until Christmas, Mommy will have plenty of time to work on my dress. She's determined it's going to be the finest dress ever. The bridesmaids need some time to get ready. Your mother wants her gardener to cut back all the poinsettias so they bloom at the right time for a reception in her garden. The wedding will be in the Lutheran Church. Your father doesn't mind. He likes our hymns."

Alice was getting out of the car by the time she finished describing the wedding plans and did not seem to notice Stephen's astonished silence. He was about to say, "No one said anything to me," when the ship's whistle blew. Captain Warner came out on deck and waved Alice aboard. Stephen barely had time to kiss her. She hugged him tightly and ran off.

The resentment Stephen had felt about his exclusion from the wedding plans, as well as his distaste for anything ostentatious, faded as he thought about Miranda's account of the accident. Thinking of what might have happened, he was grateful Alice was alive and welcomed any kind of ceremony that would bring them together.

He stopped by his father's office to report on his unsuccessful attempt to visit Lily. He was surprised to find Mark there until he remembered the scheduled business meeting with the Granard cousins. Both men looked angry.

"Lily's going to be all right," Stephen said, hoping his remark would be a distraction from whatever was troubling them.

After a pause, Mark spoke. "Karen is feeling better, too. You realize that your fiancée's thoughtless behavior might have caused Karen to have a miscarriage. Rushing in like that, covered with blood, no manners at all."

"That's it," Cedric Markham said, standing up and looking down at his two sons. "that's enough."

Stephen had never seen his father so angry nor had he ever heard him speak in such icy tones. The fury in Cedric Markham's eyes made him look like one of the avenging prophets he so often quoted.

"All I have heard from you, Mark, is what Karen feels and thinks, and not one word of concern of what happened to Lily or what might have happened to Alice," he said. *He knows*, Stephen thought. *Miranda told him about what Lily tried to do.* He continued to stare at his father.

"That was Lily's blood on the front of Alice's dress. Alice saved Lily's life, the life of the woman who was trying to kill her. And you sit there criticizing her."

"I'm sorry, Father," Mark said. "I don't understand. I don't know what you're talking about."

"You tell him, Stephen. Tell your brother how his wife's friend tried to kill Alice. I'm going outside to walk around a few minutes in the patio garden."

After his father left Stephen tried to tell Mark what had happened, just the way Miranda had told it to him. Mark looked stunned.

"I just can't believe it," he finally said.

"Well please don't tell Father you don't believe him," Stephen said. "You don't want him to have a heart attack, do you? You know what he's doing out there in the garden, don't you? He's praying, the way he always does when things don't go the way he wants. But I've never seen him this angry. Say you're sorry. Say nothing. But don't say you don't believe him."

When his father returned Mark managed to make an apology of sorts. "I'm sorry, Father. I'm sorry all this happened. It's hard to believe that Lily would do something like that."

"I've been praying for calm and understanding, but it is very difficult. It's not just Lily who has been doing the unthinkable. How dare you and your wife suggest to your mother that two Danish women should conspire together as some sort of superior beings to interfere in Stephen's marriage plans? To infer that Alice is too inferior to be part of the same family as Karen? Those were the terms used, am I correct? 'Superior'. 'Inferior'. When have those words ever been used in my household in reference to human beings created in the image of God?"

"Karen merely thought…" Mark said faltering.

"I do not care what that young woman thought. Whatever made *you* think that your mother would stoop to such a nefarious scheme? Don't you have a mind of your own?"

"We were just trying to do what Lily wanted. It was her suggestion. Karen feels very grateful to Lily."

"And you have no sense of gratitude? To your mother? Your brother? To me? I would not presume to judge in matters like these, but you and that foolish young woman have no such hesitancy. I repeat, can't you think for yourself?"

"Like Stephen, I suppose you mean."

"I didn't say that. You seem to think clearly about business." Cedric Markham was speaking more slowly, but the carefully enunciated words lost none of their force. "I only want to say this once, Mark. Your wife will behave in respectful manner to all members of this family, including Alice, or she will be no part of it. Is that clear? We are all equal in the sight of God. I have not spent my life trying to uphold Christian principles to be undermined by ignorance and deceit."

"Yes. It's clear. I'm sorry, sir. Karen meant no harm."

"I'm not so sure. I want to be sure that she doesn't cause any more trouble in the future. I expect more in the way of guidance from you as far as your wife is concerned. You are my son. And your mother's. You have lived here all your life. You should know how to behave."

Mark did look miserable and contrite. Stephen, grateful that he was not the recipient of his father's wrath, felt sorry for his brother. The pity was brief. He recalled what might have happened to Alice.

Cedric Markham resumed his seat behind the desk. After a pause during which his sons sat motionless, he spoke again in a normal tone of voice.

"Your cousin Douglas was in here earlier. He wants to concentrate on his real estate business now that the legal sale of rum is in jeopardy. The rest of the cousins should be here soon. Douglas also suggests the families get together and set up a savings and loan association to help with mortgages, land sales and such."

Grateful that the storm had passed, Stephen was willing to focus on anything other than Mark's transgression. Business transactions involving his training as a lawyer were of particular interest. Recalling his recent conversations with Beulah concerning her desire to own her own workplace and Ralph Henry's plans for laborers' housing, Stephen said that he thought mortgaging was a good idea. Mark nodded his assent.

"As a business man, I have been troubled about this threat to our economy ever since it was brought to my attention. There was no point in bothering Captain Warner with it. He was leaving and his concern was all for his sick son. But there is no doubt in my mind that the cousins are not exaggerating. Cut off from our main source of income, all of us on this island face deprivation. This is what comes of having no local government, no voice in Washington. No one can hear us. So we must try to come up with some solution of our own."

Whatever the anxieties, goals and motives of his family and friends might be, Stephen was confident that he, as a lawyer, had advantages in one area at least, that of preparing documents involving property rights. Stephen and Captain Warner often discussed the just relationship of a sovereign power to its colony, an issue that progressively troubled the Administrator. Their talks offered no clear choices.

From these ambiguities, a conviction that property rights were basic to progress emerged as Stephen tried to help people like Ralph Henry and Beulah. He was also aware of his own emotional yearning to possess land, preferably an estate like Hogansberg. If he worked with his extended family, something he had never before considered doing, he would have the chance to see that all would benefit fairly from land transfers. He could then report with pride to Alice about his struggle for social justice. The prospect filled him with excitement, the kind of emotion he sensed in Alice when she talked about the value of her work as a nurse.

"Oh, and I forgot to mention," Cedric Markham said. "Ralph Henry stopped by to say to be sure to buy the paper today. He's doing a special edition. The Armistice has been declared. The war is over, thank God. We'll be doing a special service at the Anglican Church and I imagine all the churches will do the same, offering prayers of thanks for the cessation of hostilities. I assume you both will attend services."

Stephen and Mark exchanged glances. Mark's mournful expression had changed to one of interest. *He's already thinking about entering politics and getting back in Father's good graces,* Stephen thought.

He tried desperately to remember just where on the shelves of his new office the books on real estate law were located. *A lawyer should be prepared to avoid family quarrels, prevent the collapse of friendships, and mitigate the disputes that threaten the social fabric.* That was somewhere in one of those books.

He felt closer to Alice than ever before, part of her quest to help "her people". Everyone on the island had mystical, historical or practical ties to the land that had nourished them. Many possessed all three. The visible, tangible transfer of property would affect the people far more than a conceptual transfer of national sovereignty had. When he and

Beulah had stood sided by side when the Danish flag came down and the American flag went up, their thoughts were on the social function soon to take place, who had been invited to the official reception and who had not, what new forms of discrimination might appear under American rule.

Now they both knew what transfer really meant, why some seller or buyer with philosophical insight coined the term the term "real estate". The altered landscape, the roads, the dams, made change comprehensible on everyone's level. Legality and justice were up to him. He could hardly wait to be with Alice and describe his new sense of purpose.

"These islands no longer have much military value. The Americans will see us differently, if they remember us at all." Cedric Markham said. "When we give thanks for the end of the war, we shall also pray for God's help as we face the problems of peace."

Mark said that of course he and Karen would attend services in Christiansted. Stephen, grateful for the respite from dispute, offered to accompany his father to the Anglican Church in Frederiksted. Satisfied, Cedric Markham opened the door and invited Douglas Macfarland to join them with a pleasant smile and welcoming handshake.

The maps Douglas brought with him, Stephen noted enviously, were much more professional-looking than the one he had prepared of Northside Dam. Douglas patiently pointed out the acreage that the cousins might consider selling and that which, under no circumstances, would they part with. Stephen took careful notes and promised to check on the legal ownership of the estates Douglas wanted to buy.

Rolling up his maps carefully, Douglas lingered after Cedric and Mark Markham had departed. He left the one depicting Frederiksted town district spread out on the table.

"I understand that congratulations are in order," Douglas said. "That you are unofficially engaged to marry Alice Hansen."

"It's *official*." Stephen said. "We plan to be married at Christmas time."

"Well, again, congratulations. If you just glance at this map you will see how the Markham and Hansen properties are divided only by Mahogany Road. The Hansen property is *much* larger, of course."

"Our family has always been merchants, not planters," Stephen said. "Grandfather and father never wanted the responsibility of a lot of land, just enough for a few sheep, but no cane."

"Nevertheless a sizable amount and with your father's purchase of Hogansberg you will undoubtedly become the largest landholder in Frederiksted district. You have always been rather aloof, Stephen, but like it or not, you're one of us. We can't just sit here and let the Americans take over everything. We have to get involved in self-government."

"We are under American jurisdiction."

"Oh, forget the law. I'm talking about us, the people. We want to stay the way we are, and if the Americans want to stay here, they should learn to be more like us. You, and Alice especially, are part of the landed aristocracy you've always made jokes about. You can be sure that your cousins will be there at your wedding to remind you that we're all in this together."

Printed in the United States
62421LVS00001B/1-99

9 781592 992294